D1175047

MONTANA GUNFIGHTER

MONTANA GUNFIGHTER

A WESTERN DUO

LEWIS B. PATTEN

FIVE STAR

A part of Gale, Cengage Learning

Detroit • New York • San Francisco • New Haven, Conn • Waterville, Maine • London

GALE
CENGAGE Learning™

Set in 11 pt. Plantin.
Printed on permanent paper.

LIBRARY OF CONGRESS CATALOGING-IN-PUBLICATION DATA

Patten, Lewis B.
  [Dead line]
  Montana gunfighter : a western duo / by Lewis B. Patten. — 1st ed.
    p. cm. — ("A Five Star western"—T.p. verso.)
  ISBN-13: 978-1-59414-685-5 (alk. paper)
  ISBN-10: 1-59414-685-3 (alk. paper)
    1. Western stories. I. Patten, Lewis B. Montana gunfighter. II. Title.
PS3566.A79D35 2008
813'.54—dc22   2008026786

Published in 2008 in conjunction with Golden West Literary Agency.

Printed in Mexico
2 3 4 5 6 7 12 11 10 09

CONTENTS

★ ★ ★ ★ ★

DEAD LINE

★ ★ ★ ★ ★

I

It was noon now. Midnight was the deadline. Twelve hours was little enough for a man to decide a thing like this. It wasn't enough, but it was all that remained.

Bill Roebling glanced up at the silent, two-room house. The unpainted cedar shakes that covered its walls were weathered to a dingy gray. This fall, after he'd sold a few steers, he'd planned to paint it white. He remembered a white house from his boyhood. In some odd way, white frame houses represented security and peace and happiness in his mind. Perhaps if he'd been able to paint the house before this came up. . . . He shook his head angrily. There was no solution to his problem in daydreaming about white houses. He wondered briefly whether there even was a solution, and decided reluctantly that there was not.

It boiled down to the realization that whatever he did, they would take something from him—his wife, his ranch, his self-respect, maybe his life even. By midnight tonight, one or more of these things would be gone. Again he wondered which it would be. He could imagine what Nora would be doing inside the house. She'd have her trunk out in the middle of the floor, but she wouldn't be packing. She'd be sitting in the chair beside it, staring at its gaping emptiness, wondering.

Bill was aware that upon his decision today depended his future with Nora. Nora only wanted what he guessed every woman wanted—peace. Surrender and flight would ensure the peace. But would Bill Roebling ever feel a man again afterward?

He doubted it. Over the years, could he hold a woman like Nora feeling himself but half a man? He doubted that he'd be able to.

Bill's head began to ache with the intensity of his thoughts. He was forced to admit that Nora was doing only what he himself was trying to do—to hang onto the thing she loved most. Other things fell into the background when it boiled down to a choice. Self-respect held a diminished value when placed on the scale with human life—for her, his life. The ranch became worthless when she considered that its continued possession would have to be bought so dearly.

Bill was trying to hang onto something, too, and in his mind all these things combined inextricably. Self-respect, the ranch, the cattle, Nora herself. He could not see how he could lose one without losing all. Damn them anyway! He glowered for a moment, but finally he forced himself to be calm. He forced his lagging, reluctant steps toward the house.

It was early spring. Snow lay on the north sides of the buildings. The yard was a bare expanse of trampled mud. Bill stamped his feet on the porch from old habit and automatically scraped the mud from his boots on the scraper nailed to the side of the porch.

He gazed out across the yard. Everything there had a connotation in his mind. The corral represented three weeks of work, cutting poles in the mountains twenty miles away, freighting them home with team and wagon.

The well close by the porch was two months out of his life, two months of digging like a badger while young Marcus Shoemaker hoisted the dirt out in a bucket. It represented a man's cold fear of cave-in, of being buried alive. It represented a full week of hauling rocks with which to shore up its walls.

The barn, dug into a bank facing the dry bed of the creek, was another month of grueling labor, and a source of pride. It was roofed with cedar poles laid side-by-side and covered with brush. Green sod overlaid the brush to make it tight. Its front was open, facing the south.

Bill opened the door and stepped into the kitchen. He took off his hat and stood hesitantly for a moment.

Bill Roebling was a big, patient man. His mouth was a wide, good-humored slash in his dark-tanned face. His hair was the color of prairie grass in winter, his eyes the slate gray of the sky when a haze of storm lies across it. Eyes that could be gentle, eyes that could be hard as granite. He glanced toward his wife.

As he had guessed, her trunk sat, empty and open, in the center of the bedroom. Nora sat on the edge of the bed. She did not look at him, but he could tell that she was aware of his presence.

The stiffness in her admitted that this decision was his. Yet she feared that his decision and the one she wanted him to make would not be the same. She was afraid Bill would be stubborn, and she knew, if he was, he would die.

Less accusing than disappointed, he said: "You haven't got much faith, have you, Nora?"

She looked up at him. She was beautiful, even when angry, even when that chill look of withdrawal was in her normally soft and laughing eyes. Her hair was black as night, and as velvety soft. Her skin reminded Bill of strawberries and cream. Her lips were full and ripe, and so was her body. But the sight of her could stir no hot excitement in Bill today.

She laughed bitterly. There was hurt in her eyes, and awful fear. "Faith in one man who doesn't even own a gun against Henry McCambridge? Against Cheyenne Robbins?" She laughed again, but it sounded more like a sob than a laugh. "You're asking more of me than faith, Bill."

He said: "Maybe they're bluffing. Maybe all it would take would be one man who would stand fast."

"How long will you stand fast with a bullet in you?" She stared at him, the cruelty of her own words seeping into her consciousness. Briefly her expression softened.

Bill took a step toward her, and quickly she showed him that coldness that he could never penetrate. He stopped. Nora said: "No. Don't come near me. Don't touch me. Don't think you can ever turn me soft again."

Weariness flowed through Bill Roebling. He said dully: "I'll go over to Shoemaker's, and Tully's, and Welch's. I'll get some help."

She did not look at him, nor did she speak. He turned toward the door and said harshly: "Pack that damned trunk or put it away. Don't sit there looking at it."

He went outside into the steaming sunlight, slamming the door behind him. The land stretched away from the tiny house, mile on mile of it. Enough, you would think, for men to enjoy and live upon in peace.

Well, he hated asking help from his neighbors, but it was their fight as well as his. If McCambridge drove Bill Roebling out, it would be but the beginning. All the others would have to go, too.

He crossed the yard to the corral. He caught his horse and threw up the weathered old hull that served him as a saddle. A persistent feeling of depression dogged him as he rode away. When a woman lost faith in a man, she took something from him. She took a measure of his confidence.

MC Bar sprawled over a full ten acres of ground. Its rambling house had room for half a dozen families and housed only one. Its barn could hold two hundred cattle and seldom held over a dozen horses. Its range land could support thirty thousand cattle, and McCambridge had only four thousand. Yet he was driving small cowmen and settlers off the grass. He had let

Cheyenne Robbins talk him into it. He was a big man, and he had lots of power and arrogance. But only Cheyenne Robbins knew that his strength was Cheyenne's strength, that his power was in Cheyenne Robbins's gun. Without Robbins, he would be a big man with a lot of bluster and little else.

Robbins was about forty-five. He'd been at MC Bar for nearly ten years now. He was a slim man, almost skinny. His face was seamed, his eyes as bright and hot and black as Nora Roebling's hair.

Nora. Robbins dismounted, thinking of her. He watched Mc-Cambridge's bulky figure as it strode toward the house. He handed his reins to a kid who came slouching from the bunkhouse, and then went toward the one-room log cabin that was the foreman's quarters on MC Bar.

He was frowning, not entirely happy with the way things had gone. He had expected to see Bill Roebling break, had, in fact, counted on this. He had figured that, if Bill Roebling broke, that Nora would lose her stubborn respect for her marriage vows.

Cheyenne Robbins respected only power and strength, and he supposed that women respected the same virtues. Cheyenne had seen many women he wanted, yet never had he wanted one with the maddening and abiding passion with which he wanted Nora Roebling. He had become a frequent visitor at Roebling's place while Bill was away riding, until finally Nora had told him bluntly not to come back. It had angered him, of course, until his everlasting male ego came to his rescue. Now he believed that Nora nurtured a secret longing for him, that she was repulsing him only because of her marriage vows, because she valued the respect of the community.

His ego had driven him to talk McCambridge into driving the settlers away. Now, his ego supported his idea that he could kill Bill Roebling at midnight, and, later, after the hullabaloo had died away, win Nora easily. But it meant waiting. Perhaps it even meant leaving MC Bar and this country that would know she was Bill Roebling's widow and Cheyenne, Bill's killer.

No, Cheyenne was not pleased with the way things had gone. And a slow-growing, murderous anger began to build from the frustration in him. He sat down and rolled himself a wheat-straw cigarette. He touched a match to its end and, when it didn't draw right, tossed it viciously to the floor.

It made little difference now, what Bill Roebling decided to do. The end would be the same. Cheyenne Robbins had no intention of allowing him to leave and to take Nora with him. Bill Roebling had to die.

Shoemaker's place nestled in a small hollow. It had a better spring than did Bill's small ranch. The spring seeped out of the hillside and ran for a full half mile before it disappeared into the ground. Bill decided that McCambridge should have wanted Shoemaker's place even more than he wanted Bill's.

He scowled. He fished his big silver watch from his pocket and looked at the time. 1:30 p.m. Shrugging, he rode into Shoemaker's yard. He guessed there was a reason for McCambridge's decision to tackle Bill first. Bill was alone. Shoemaker had two sons, both nearly grown. They'd be handled easier if McCambridge could set the pattern with Bill, could make Bill Roebling back water and run first.

Shoemaker was up on the roof of a sod outbuilding. His sons stood in a wagon below and threw dirt up onto the roof while the old man spread it with a shovel.

Bill rode his horse close to the wagon. Shoemaker was a tall, gaunt man. His expression was grave, almost melancholy. He nodded at Bill. "Howdy. Git down an' set a spell."

His two sons were but younger editions of the old man. Both were tall and skinny. Their wrists were red and bony, sticking out of the sleeves of their identical, outgrown flannel shirts. They worked with steady concentration. Their failure to meet Bill's eyes gave him an odd feeling of uneasiness, and he knew by it that they had heard of McCambridge's ultimatum.

Bill said: "McCambridge and that hardcase foreman of his were over this morning early."

Shoemaker, on the roof, nodded. His gray beard, so carefully combed, made him look wise and patriarchal. It hid a large part of his facial expression, at times making him seem inscrutable. He said: "I know. Lucius here saw them ride past."

He kept spreading the dirt carefully, too carefully. Bill had the feeling that Shoemaker knew what Cheyenne wanted at Bill Roebling's place. He said with some asperity: "Did Lucius read Cheyenne's mind as he went past? You act like you knew what he wanted."

Shoemaker shrugged. "What did he want?"

"My place. He gave me until midnight to get out."

Shoemaker's eyes showed his surprise. It puzzled Bill. Shoemaker hesitated for a moment, then he laid aside his shovel and climbed laboriously from the roof. His joints quite obviously pained him. It was rheumatism, and he'd been this way for a long time, as long as Bill could remember.

Shoemaker asked: "You came over here for something. What is it?"

Bill was puzzled again by his taciturnity, by the hooded secretiveness of his eyes. He said: "Why, I guess you know what I want. I want some help. I don't want to leave."

Shoemaker chose his words carefully. He said: "We want to be good neighbors, but we're farmin' men, not fightin' men. We got one gun betwixt us, and the boys have never even fired it. When we fust come here, I used to kill me an antelope once in a while." He lifted his blue eyes to Bill's. They showed Bill smoldering anger, and a righteous resentment. "You asking me

15

to bring my boys and that old gun and face up to Cheyenne Robbins?"

Bill said stubbornly: "If you don't, and they drive me out, then you'll be next. McCambridge ain't going to be satisfied with just my place. He's only making a test out of me."

Shoemaker stared at Bill. He said: "By the Lord Harry, you believe that, don't you?"

"Sure. I . . . wouldn't say it if I didn't." He frowned, not understanding Shoemaker at all. "What the hell are you trying to say, Shoemaker?"

Shoemaker kept his eyes on the ground. His chin turned stubborn and his mouth firmed out. He said: "I wouldn't be an honest man if I didn't tell you. Today ain't the fust time Cheyenne's been over to your place. Only always before it's been when you ain't to home."

The effect of his words was like a kick in the belly to Bill. They made that same emptiness grow there, that same nausea. Shoemaker stepped back and picked up a grubbing hoe. He was ready when Bill's rage hit him. Bill took a step toward the old man, but Shoemaker raised the hoe in a threatening manner. Bill could hear the slight noises Lucius and Marcus made getting down off the wagon.

Shoemaker said soothingly: "Sure you're mad. Anybody'd be. But don't take it out on me, man."

Bill said scathingly: "Shoemaker, you've got a dirty mind. If you was some younger, I'd take that hoe away from you and beat you to death with it." He let his eyes rest coldly on the older man for a few moments. Then he turned on his heel.

His anger was a slow burning fire within him. His first reaction was to blame Shoemaker with inventing the tale so that he could avoid becoming involved. But that did not check with what Bill knew of the man. No, if Shoemaker said he believed the story, then he really believed it.

He swung up to his saddle and rode away, not even bothering to speak again, or to look back. He was human enough to wonder briefly if there was any truth in Shoemaker's accusation.

He was instantly ashamed of his own doubt. And anger had a way of growing within him because of both the doubt and the shame. He told himself emphatically: *Nora's done nothing she shouldn't have done! Another thought occurred to him: But maybe Cheyenne's jumping me instead of one of the others more because of Nora than because of the ranch.*

Well, Shoemaker was not the only one to whom he could go for help. There was Tully. Bill suspected Tully of helping himself to an occasional two or three cows that wore the MC Bar brand, but he had no proof. Neither did McCambridge have proof, or Tully wouldn't still be around.

Bill looked at his watch. 2:00 p.m. Ten hours to go. The resolution to stay and fight it out was growing in Bill Roebling. All that still held him hesitant was Nora. He was increasingly afraid that, if he stayed and fought, Nora would go anyway. He could not forget that coldness that had been in her, that coldness that had been almost unfriendly. Again the doubt assailed him. Maybe that was just what Cheyenne Robbins was playing for. Maybe he was trying to separate Bill and Nora so that he could have Nora. Bill laughed bitterly. It hurt his ego to think that a scrawny, aging man like Robbins could be pleasing to Nora. So he refused to believe it. Nora was his, or had been until today. She would be his again when midnight was past. Or Bill Roebling would be dead. He shook his head impatiently. Did he really intend to fight, or was he just deluding himself? What if Tully and Welch both refused him their help?

He was beginning to feel the strain of indecision. It would be easier, he guessed, if he made a hard and fast decision now. He could either say no, and let them do what they would, or he could tuck his tail between his legs, pack up, and leave. There were only two ways out of this, really. Unless he could get some support from the other small cowmen and nesters. Or unless he could get some backing from the law.

There was no road between Shoemaker's and Tully's, but Bill knew the way. He pointed his horse toward Tully's greasy, bachelor shack, his head sunk down in deep thought upon his chest.

Henry McCambridge and his scrawny foreman had come riding into Roebling's yard early this morning. He had had his milking done, and his breakfast finished. He was standing in the yard, idly picking his teeth with a sharpened matchstick, trying to decide whether to spend the day riding, or whether it was more important that he spend it beginning the smokehouse that Nora wanted. McCambridge was a big man, standing six feet two without the extra height his cowman's boots gave him. He was solid through the chest and growing a rounded paunch from age and good living. He had the graying, arrogant look that ordinary men who come to success by their own efforts so often achieve. He wore a long mustache that was also gray. He was smoking a cigar. He took it out of his mouth long enough to say shortly: "Cheyenne tells me we been losin' too many cows. I made up my mind the only way to stop it is to get rid of you damned squatters. You're first, Roebling."

Bill was highly irritated by the other's haughty assurance, by his roughshod tone. "What the hell do you mean, I'm first? I got my own cows. I live here. I hold my land by the same right you hold yours. I run my cattle on the Public Domain, same as you do. Do you think I'm going to leave because some damned fool tells me to?"

McCambridge sat his big sorrel without a change of expression. But his voice mirrored a certain doubt. He said: "You talk to him, Robbins." He rode away, but he halted his horse about a quarter mile from the house.

Cheyenne rolled a chew of tobacco from one cheek to the other. He had bright, flat eyes that were nearly black. They mirrored now a hot wickedness of soul; they showed Bill anticipation that was almost gleeful. He said: "The boss means that, if you stay, you stay underground. That plain enough?"

Bill Roebling's big, work-roughened hands opened and closed spasmodically. He could break this little diamond-back between them easily. But while he was doing it, he'd get stung by the man's blue-steel fangs. He could feel the blood draining out of his face, could feel the vast emptiness in his stomach. He made his eyes hold Robbins's glance unflinchingly, even though he knew that too much defiance might earn him a bullet. He wondered briefly if Robbins would gun him down right here, unarmed, with no chance at all. He decided that Robbins would, and it gave him a little caution. But he said: "You expect a man to take something like that with no notice at all? You crowd too hard. I won't say right now. You tell McCambridge I'll think on it. Ain't he even offering to buy me out?"

"No." Robbins laughed. "Nothin' for the place. He'll buy your cattle if you want to sell 'em. Ten dollars a head."

Bill Roebling stared. "Ten dollars? They're worth thirty."

"Ten." Robbins stared at him.

It was this way, then, with no pretense at fairness. It was a boot in your backside and to hell with your feelings if they got hurt. It was to make a man know he was a coward if he ran and a fool if he didn't.

Robbins stirred his feet in the stirrups and the horse turned. Over his shoulder he called: "Midnight! I'll be back at midnight. You be packed and ready to leave, you hear?" He was grinning. One of his yellowed front teeth was broken off and capped clumsily with bullet lead.

He said a few words to McCambridge and the two rode away. Bill gave up all notion of working today and went to the house. Nora looked up from her sweeping, concern showing in her eyes, momentarily ignoring the visit of McCambridge and Robbins. "Going to start my smokehouse today?"

He shook his head. Nora asked in a small voice: "What did they want?"

Bill rolled a smoke with hands that shook. Still he found it hard to believe. The ultimatum had come like a bolt of lightning out of a clear blue sky. His voice, when he spoke, held a certain outrage. "They served notice on me that it was leave or take the consequences." He'd started to say—". . . get killed."—but changed it at the last instant.

Nora's face paled. She would not meet his eyes. This was not exactly a surprise to either of them. You sensed these things brewing long before they happened. There was talk in town; there was the thinly veiled hostility between McCambridge and the squatters.

"How much did they offer you?" Nora asked.

"Nothing for the place. Ten dollars for the cattle."

He saw momentarily what he'd hoped he'd see. A firming of her pretty jaw line. A quickened rise and fall of her breasts. A spark of raw anger in her eyes. But it was quickly gone. Apathy settled where the anger had been. Apathy and hopelessness, and new, growing terror.

She said: "Bill, we'll go. How long do we have?"

"Midnight," he said. "And I haven't decided to go."

"But it's all you can do. Cheyenne Robbins is vicious. He'll kill you if you don't."

So they argued. Bill had to admit that Nora had a voice in the decision. But he felt she was making her decision on purely emotional grounds, and he felt that was wrong. They argued until coldness came between them, she stubbornly sticking to her original stand, he refusing to decide anything until he had weighed all the possibilities.

Now he rode across the empty land toward the greasy sack outfit that Tully owned. He pictured Tully in his mind. A small, dirty man with an ingratiating, almost cowering manner. Tully was like an oft-whipped dog, crawling toward you, tail wagging, tongue lolling, expecting a kick or a blow, but begging for something else. He hardly ever shaved, and Bill suspected that he seldom washed. Bill hated to ask anything of him. But in this, he had no choice. Shoemaker had bluntly refused to help. And Bill had to have someone.

II

Around noon, Cheyenne Robbins left the MC Bar and rode back along the route to Roebling's place. All morning he had lain on his bunk and fretted. He began to fear that this would get away from him. He began to doubt if killing Bill Roebling would get him Roebling's wife. He even began to doubt if showing Bill up for a coward would turn his wife against him. He began to doubt his own ego, his own assurance, and it rubbed at his nerve ends all morning, until he could lie still no longer.

At about 1:30 p.m. he dropped over a slight rise of ground and saw the little two-room house before him. He dismounted at the corral, and went toward the house. His knock brought a tearful Nora to the door.

She cried angrily: "Go away! Bill isn't here, but we're going! Does that satisfy you? Is that what you wanted? You couldn't make love to me behind Bill's back, so this is your revenge. Well, I hope you're enjoying it!"

He said uneasily, lying because he sensed that was all that would help him now: "Nora, I couldn't help it. It ain't my idea, it's McCambridge's. I've been at MC Bar for ten years. Am I supposed to throw all that overboard for your husband?"

"Yes, if it's wrong!"

"What good would that do? McCambridge would still drive the settlers off, your husband among them." He could sense that his argument had half convinced her. He said urgently: "Nora, I love you. I want you. If. . . ." He stopped. Even in his mind, the suggestion had a harsh sound, a bargaining sound.

But Nora asked: "If what?"

"If I turn against McCambridge and stand with your husband, what then?"

Her eyes widened with shock. There was a sort of horror in them. Her voice was barely audible. "What are you trying to say? Are you suggesting that you'll let Bill alone if I'll . . . ?" She couldn't finish. A light shudder ran through her.

Cheyenne had intended to marry Nora if he got the chance. Now, maybe he wouldn't have to. He licked his thin lips, and nodded.

All color had drained from Nora's face. She said: "Get out of here! Get out!"

Cheyenne's lips drew away from his teeth. His eyes glittered, and his face flushed with anger. He took a step toward her.

But Nora was quicker. She slammed the door and dropped the bar across it. She stood with her back to the door for a moment, shaking. Cheyenne pounded upon its thick panels with the butt of his gun, cursing obscenely.

Nora waited until the pounding stopped, then went to the window and peered out. She hoped he didn't get the idea of forcing his way in through the window. She looked across the room at the cast-iron skillet on the back of the stove. She felt tainted and unclean, almost as though she had allowed Cheyenne to touch her. Then she saw him striding away across the yard. She went into the bedroom and looked at her trunk. She sat down on the bed and stared at its gaping emptiness.

It was fantastic, incredible. Robbins was threatening Bill solely because of her. Suddenly, frantically Nora Roebling began to pack.

The only thing on Tully's place that was worth anything was its corral. This morning it held two horses. Tully came to the door in a pair of baggy pants and no shirt. His underwear was a faded red. He grinned warily and raised his hand in uncertain greeting. He was not used to visits from his neighbors.

Bill swung to the ground. His horse, released, wandered toward the corral and stuck his nose between the poles to nuzzle curiously at the horses inside.

Tully said: "Don't see you much over this way. Come on in."

Bill went into the untidy shack. It smelled of stale bedding. A pot of coffee simmered on the back of the stove. Tully wiped out a tin cup with a greasy rag and poured it full, then handed it to Bill. Bill didn't want it, but he didn't want to refuse it, either. He sipped it for politeness' sake.

He noticed the double-barreled shotgun that was propped in a corner, a Winchester .30-30 beside it. He noticed the Colt .45 in its holster hung over the back of a chair. Of all the small ranchers and nesters in this country, it appeared that Tully was the best armed. Bill wondered if Tully could stand up to Robbins and decided that he could not. Effectiveness against the gunman was not so much a matter of armament as courage and stamina. Bill doubted if Tully's guns would do him much good, because Tully wouldn't use them, and Robbins would know that he wouldn't. Suddenly he wished he hadn't come. He hated to ask anything of Tully.

Tully said: "Grass's turnin' green. Be a good year." He was cautious, for he sensed the trouble that was in Bill's mind, also sensed that Bill had come to ask a favor of some kind.

Bill nodded. He gathered his muscles to get up. He set the

tin cup among the dirty dishes on the rickety table. He stood up, but he didn't go. He thought of Nora.

He said: "McCambridge and Robbins have got the pressure on me. I've got until midnight to leave."

The grin faded from Tully's seamed and whiskered face. His eyes grew cautious. He whistled softly. "Why you?' I figgered they'd be after me fust."

Bill could have told him why. Driving Tully from the country would have made no impression on the honest settlers. They would have misunderstood, would have thought that McCambridge's desire to be rid of Tully was based upon Tully's undoubted but unproved rustling activities. Tully's turn was coming. But Bill suspected that Tully wouldn't be driven away. He'd be hung.

Bill was still holding the conviction in his mind that he'd been right, that Shoemaker had been wrong about MC Bar's motive in wanting to be rid of Bill Roebling. He said: "I don't know why they picked me to start things off. But you can see how it will affect the rest of you, can't you? I'm just the starter. He'll pick us off one by one. Unless we get together and show him a solid front."

Tully stuck his face close to Bill's. His breath was rank and sour, his expression knowing and unpleasant. He said: "McCambridge don't want my layout. But he wants yours, and his foreman wants your wife. You ain't goin' to pull me into this, my friend. No, siree. McCambridge would like a good excuse for killin' me. I ain't about to give it to him." He stepped back, and his lips snarled. "You get out of here an' leave me alone! You just keep me out of your ruckus with MC Bar."

Bill Roebling could feel his anger rising. He could feel the growth of humiliation. He wanted to hit Tully for his insinuation about Nora. He shrugged, not even trying to grin. "All right. I just thought I'd ask."

24

He was sick inside. He got out the door as quickly as he could, leaving Tully muttering resentfully behind him. He kicked the notion around in his head of asking Tully for the loan of that shotgun. But he'd had enough humiliation at Tully's hands. He strode swiftly to the corral and climbed on his horse.

Out of sight of Tully's, he halted the animal. Now where? Well, there was Ross Welch yet. And there were a few other settlers, but most of them were the sodbuster variety, like Shoemaker. Not fighting men, farming men. He wondered if everyone in the country knew about Cheyenne Robbins's yen for Nora. He was angered anew because Nora had told him nothing of it. He had to admit, however, that it had probably been only concern for Bill's own safety that had kept her silent. She knew that Bill had a temper. She had been afraid he might start trouble with Cheyenne and get killed for his pains.

Sour and discouraged, Bill Roebling set out for Ross Welch's place. Ross was a young man, less than thirty. He had done some fighting in his younger years. His woman, Katie, had settled him down.

Bill Roebling had gone to school with Katie. He suspected she would have married him if he'd asked her. But he'd found Nora, and after that hadn't even been able to see Katie. Ross Welch fought the tight curb bit Katie kept in his mouth, sometimes. Maybe he'd welcome the thought of a scrap.

Feeling better, Bill lifted his horse to a lope. Welch's place was over at the foot of the mountains, nestling in a small, watered draw. He had a hay meadow of about sixty acres, but for the rest he made his living from a small bunch of cattle and from working out whenever the chance presented itself. Sometimes he cut and hauled cedar posts for McCambridge.

The land flowed past, and again Bill Roebling had the sensation of time rushing by. He looked at his watch, recognizing the growing nervousness in himself. Hell, he had plenty of time yet.

It was only 3:00 p.m. He still had nine hours.

It was a long ride to Welch's place. An hour and a half ride. The watch said 4:30 p.m. when Bill rode into the yard. He dismounted and looped his reins around the low branch of a willow tree. He tramped toward the house from whose chimney a thin plume of smoke arose. Ross was not in evidence in the yard. Perhaps Katie could tell Bill where he could be found.

He knocked on the door. Katie answered it. The kitchen was steamy from a copper boiler of clothes simmering on the stove. Bill heard a thin, fretful wail of a baby from the open bedroom.

Katie cried: "Bill! Where'd you drop from?" Holding her hands behind her, she reached up and gave him a kiss on the cheek. Bill felt embarrassed. He stood just inside the door, with his hat awkwardly twisting in his hands.

Katie Welch was a small woman. Her hair was a copper red. She seemed to have faded and aged in the last two years. But she was still pretty, and excitement at seeing him put a happy glow upon her face. Bill asked: "Where's Ross, Katie?"

"He's looking for one of his cows. She was springing, and was kind of thin after the winter. He's afraid she's gone off to have her calf and somehow got into trouble with it."

"You got any idea when he'll be back?"

She shook her head. "Can I help, Bill?"

"No. But I thought maybe Ross would."

"What's the matter?"

He tried to smile. "It's McCambridge and Robbins. They're moving me out. I figure they're going to move everybody out. McCambridge said he's been losing too many cattle, and he blames all of us for it."

Katie laughed harshly. "Why doesn't he go after the man that's guilty? Everybody knows Tully is the one that's to blame for that."

"I guess it isn't a question really of losing cows. McCambridge is a range hog. He can't use it all, but he doesn't want anybody else on it."

"And you want Ross to help." It was a statement. Bill thought her face paled a little as she said it. He nodded.

The baby in the bedroom uttered a piercing wail, and Katie excused herself hurriedly and went in to him. Ross stared around at the cluttered kitchen. After a few moments, Katie came out, carrying the child, which could not have been over six months old. She held him up to Bill, and Bill self-consciously poked his chin with a careful forefinger.

He had the feeling again of time flowing swiftly past. It was not yet 5:00 p.m. Ross probably wouldn't return until 6:00 or after. And then Bill would have the long ride into town ahead of him. He knew it was useless to try to find Ross. There were a hundred small draws that could hide a single rider. And Bill was not familiar with the country.

He said: "They've given me until midnight. If Ross is going to help, he'll have to be at my place before them. Will you ask him, Katie?"

"Of course I will, Bill."

A certain constraint seemed to grow up between them then. It was as if Katie recognized the seriousness of this, and was feeling resentment because Bill sought to involve her husband. Bill knew a feeling of guilt. He really had no right even to ask this of Ross. Particularly if he was wrong about the reason behind his orders to move. He consoled himself with the conviction—*If our situations were reversed, I'd help Ross.*—but he could not help wondering if Nora would have let him. And he could not help wondering if Katie would tell Ross that he'd been here.

He said, turning: "Thanks, Katie. I figured I could count on Ross and you." He opened the door and stepped outside. After the steamy kitchen, the air was raw and cold. He said, in parting: "You folks drop in when you're over our way."

Katie smiled at him strangely. "And you come back, Bill."

Bill Roebling untied his horse, and swung into the saddle. He heard the door slam across the yard. He rode out, feeling no lift in his spirits at all. He felt that he could count on Ross Welch. Why, then, did he continue to be so depressed?

Katie closed the door before Bill had ridden out, for she held the baby in her arms, and the draft from the open door was cold and raw. From the window she watched Bill ride away. His shoulders were not squared and straight as they usually were. They were slumped with discouragement. Katie watched him until he went out of sight over a low rise. Her expression was pensive, her eyes oddly soft. There was no denying it. She had loved Bill Roebling before. She loved him still. But a woman, by the time she became an adult, learned that with life you must make compromises. She might have had Bill if she'd played it differently. But she hadn't. And instead of Bill, she had Ross. She might think of Bill sometimes. She might imagine that the lean, hard frame beside her in bed was Bill instead of Ross. But that was as far as it would ever go.

She sat down in a chair, loosened her dress, and nursed the baby. He was sleeping when she got up and carried him back into, the bedroom. He was a pretty child, and for a moment she stood looking down at him. His hair, what there was of it, was as black as Ross's. His eyes had changed, almost unnoticed, from their baby blue to brown, like his father's.

Katie set the clothes boiler off the stove and began to prepare supper. A light frown came to her forehead and stayed there. Her eyes were worried and full of uncertainty. She had promised Bill that she would ask Ross to help him. Now she began to wonder if she really would. If Ross rode over to Roebling's tonight, he might not come back. Katie knew Cheyenne Robbins's reputation as well as anyone in the country. She knew he could be cruel and ruthless. She hated him, but she was afraid of him, too. Also, she doubted if McCambridge's greed extended this far. This place was nearly fifteen miles from MC Bar.

Yet she knew as well that the decision as to whether Ross would go or not depended entirely on her. He would go if she told him Bill needed help. Ross was half wild, and would go because he liked a fight if for no other reason. Perhaps that was why she hesitated. There was no restraint in Ross when the smell of conflict was upon him. Katie let herself think of what it would be like, alone, without Ross. She let herself consider what the baby could expect of life without a father to grow up with him.

Reversing herself, she considered Bill Roebling, pictured him standing against McCambridge and Cheyenne Robbins. And at last she came to her decision: *If Ross doesn't go, there will be no fighting. Bill will lose his place, but no one will lose their lives.*

Ross came in at 6:00 p.m., cold and tired, and hugged her boisterously. She set his supper before him, oddly worried, oddly quiet. She wished she could know that her decision was right. She wished she could face the future without this uneasy feeling that if Bill died, she alone would be responsible.

Dusk lay over the high plains when Bill sighted Tully's place again in the distance. All the way from Welch's, he had known an increasing depression, for he understood now that Katie would say nothing to Ross when he came in. And perhaps that was right. It was not to be doubted that Welch might escape the greed of McCambridge and Robbins. It was also questionable if one man had the right to ask of another that he risk his life.

So he could cross Shoemaker and Tully and Welch off his list. And it was now too late to see any of the others. Besides that, Bill doubted if he would get any better response from the others than he had from the three he'd visited.

He nearly passed Tully's without coming near enough to be seen, but then he remembered the double-barreled shotgun leaning in the corner of the dirty shack.

One thing was sure. If he were to buck Robbins, he would need a gun.

So reluctantly he reined his horse over, and approached the shack from which a single light gleamed.

Coming into the yard, he hailed the house. "Tully! Hey, you there?" He knew a man with the burden Tully carried upon his conscience might well shoot an intruder first and ask questions afterward.

Tully came to the door, sour and gruff. "What the hell you want now? I thought I told you. . . ."

"You did." It was all Bill could do to keep from blowing up. Suddenly he hoped the time would come someday when he would never need to ask a favor from anybody again. He went on: "I need a gun. I figured maybe you'd loan me that shotgun."

Tully snorted. "It won't do you no good."

Bill said patiently: "Let me borrow it anyway."

Tully said: "It's worth twenty dollars. What if you git killed?"

Bill wasn't in the habit of carrying money, not unless he was headed for town. He had none on him today. He said: "I'll buy it. I haven't got any money with me today, but I'll give you an I.O.U. If anything happens to me, Nora'll give you the money."

Tully shook his head. Bill figured this was just giving him an excuse to refuse. The horse Bill was riding was a big bay animal, deep of chest, strong of leg. A horse that would carry a man all day and herd a steer when the day was done. The bay was worth $50 any day of the week. Bill shifted in his saddle. He said: "I'll give you a bill of sale for this horse. You can come after him tomorrow morning."

Greed fought with Tully's desire to refuse plainly in the man's sharp face. But the trade was too good to refuse. Bill had known it would be.

Tully growled: "All right. Come in and write it out."

Bill dismounted wearily. The strain of the day was beginning to make itself felt. He went into the stinking cabin, and Tully handed him a scrap of paper and a pencil. Bill wrote out the bill of sale and put the date below his signature.

He started for the door, but Tully said: "Win, lose, or draw, the hoss's mine. Understand?"

"All right." He picked up the shotgun, broke the action, and peered through the barrels at the lamp. There was some rust there, but the gun would shoot. $10 would have hit its value closer than $20, but when a man had to have something, he didn't haggle. Bill said: "How many shells you got?"

Tully got out a box. It was a little more than half full. He handed it to Bill reluctantly, and Bill could almost smile, so obvious was the greed on the little man's face. Tully was considering asking an exorbitant price for the shells as well as for the gun. Shame must have stirred him at the last minute. He said wryly: "Double O buckshot. A good load for men. With the two barrels you can kill five men at fifteen feet." Bill grunted: "I need something to even the odds." With that, he turned the horse and rode away. But as he turned, he caught the bright, possessive gleam in Tully's eyes as they ran over the tall horse. He could imagine what Nora would have to say about this, trading as good a horse as he'd ever owned for a rusty shotgun. Thinking of Nora brought that aspect of his trouble freshly before his mind. He guessed Nora would have her trunk packed by now. She would be waiting for him to come home and hitch up the wagon. Maybe she would have already done it herself. Maybe she was even now driving toward town.

He shrugged sourly, and the anger that had lain dormant in him all afternoon began to grow anew. Bill didn't try to check it. But neither did he try to fan it higher. He was aware that he could not hold a sustained rage from now until midnight. And at midnight, he knew that, if he was to stand up to Cheyenne Robbins, he would have to be mad—good and mad.

He pointed the tired horse toward town and hurried him slightly with his insistent heels. It must be about 6:30 p.m. now. It would be 7:30 before he could reach town, 9:00 or 9:30 before he could get back home.

Home! He wondered if the house would be dark when he finally did arrive. He wondered if Nora would still be there. He doubted it. And he began to wonder what there would be to fight for if she wasn't.

The miles fell behind slowly and steadily. Bill was a patient man. But the day had been too long. Any day was too long to carry what Bill had carried in his mind today. And still he could not tell himself definitely what his stand would be. His mind was still undecided. He would have to talk to Jan Lederer, the sheriff, before he would have all the ingredients for a decision.

III

Deep darkness lay over the town as Bill Roebling entered its outskirts. He rode up the single street, and before the hotel swung to the ground. He tied the weary horse and climbed the two steps to the boardwalk. The sheriff's office, close against the hotel, was dark. Bill went into the hotel, and peered about the lobby.

He did not see the sheriff here, so he went on through into the bar. Jan Lederer stood with a heel hooked over the bar rail. He was talking to the fat, pink-faced bartender.

Bill Roebling could remember when saloons and bars had been as familiar to him as the feel of a saddle under his thighs. But that had been two years ago. He hadn't had a drink of whiskey since he'd married Nora. He hadn't needed whiskey. Nora had been stimulation enough for any man.

Uncertainty gripped him as he stared at the sheriff. Lederer was a stocky, middle-aged man. His eyes were hard and cold under his bushy gray brows. His mouth was equally hard, not given to much smiling. These were the marks of character on the sheriff's face, but Bill Roebling knew the marks lied. The sheriff was not hard. He was calculating and careful. Bill began to doubt if he'd get much support from Lederer.

He approached the man, who was alone at the bar. A couple of MC Bar cowpunchers were playing whist at a wall table. The bartender turned an inquiring eye on Bill, but Bill shook his head, saying: "Nothing for me. I want to talk to the sheriff."

Lederer gave him a thin smile. "What about?"

"McCambridge and Robbins. They've given me until midnight to move out." He could see the swift evasion in the sheriff's eyes, the groping for a legitimate excuse. He said: "I want you to ride out there with me. I want you there when they come back at midnight."

Lederer grunted: "They're bluffing, boy. They won't bother you."

"The hell they won't! You coming or not?"

"They ain't done nothing yet. I can't move until they break the law." His attitude was withdrawn, cautious, unfriendly.

Suddenly all the frustration of the day burst over the dam of Bill's control. He said softly and maliciously: "You're a god-damned liar, Sheriff. The only trouble with you is the yellow streak that runs along your spine."

The sheriff could move fast for all his stocky bulk. His left arm shoved him away from the bar, while his right swung in a tight arc and exploded on the side of Bill Roebling's jaw. Bill staggered back, a third of the way to the door before he recovered. The sheriff was on him like a wolf, his fists driving in with short, punishing blows like a pair of steam pistons. Bill took them for a minute, letting the shock and pain of them raise his anger, raise the day's resentment to a kind of flaming fury. Then he let go of a couple of his own. His left caught the sheriff flat on the mouth, and Bill felt teeth give before his knuckles. His right caught Lederer along the left side of his jaw bone.

The sheriff staggered back until the bar stopped him. Bill moved in to finish this, but the voice of the bartender brought him up short: "Hold that!"

He shifted his eyes to the gaping barrel of the bartender's short shotgun. It rested, steady and implacable, on the top of the bar, lined exactly on Bill Roebling's chest. Bill dropped his hands and shrugged. He started to turn, but the bartender said: "Wait." He turned to Lederer and asked: "You want this one in jail, Jan?"

Bill said: "Better not try it or you'll have to use that shotgun. I don't think you want to do that." He turned his back and went to the door. There, he paused insolently for an instant before he went through it. He came into the street, untied his horse, and mounted wearily. His heels dug into the animal's ribs and the horse moved sluggishly downstreet.

Bill's mouth was swelling, and so was one of his eyes. Leaving town, darkness closed like a cloak over him. Only the stars put light upon the landscape, and that was barely enough so that a man could see the road.

Bill was hungry now, and he was cold. He shivered slightly. The fight and anger in him began to fade, leaving only the residue of weariness, hopelessness, and disillusionment. He rode for a full hour before he heard the sound of hoofs ahead, and the familiar *creak* of his own wagon. He pulled off the road, far enough so that he would be unseen. He muffled the bay's nostrils with his hand, although he doubted if the horse had enough energy left in him to nicker.

He heard the wagon go past, and he could see the blur of Nora's slight shape at the reins. Now, at last, he knew that he was truly alone. The knowledge came to him with a definite shock. He held the horse still for a full five minutes after Nora had passed. For the first time today he began to wonder how much truth there was to Shoemaker's story. What the hell was the use now? Nora was gone. He had no friends. His ranch, when you evaluated it in terms of coldly material things, was of little consequence, hardly worth fighting over.

What, then, held him here? What kept him from turning his horse back toward town, from following Nora, from going where he wanted to go? He knew, at last, what it was. Pride. She had quit him when the going got rough for him. He'd not go crawling to her. He could never love her again after this, no matter what happened. He narrowed it down. If pride and the shreds of self-respect were all that were left, then he'd hold to them until the very end. His anger, dormant all day, began to rise by leaps and bounds. His decision had been made for him. They'd crowded him just a little too hard.

He reached home and put his horse into the corral. Tully's horse now. He took the shotgun into the house, and carefully loaded both barrels. He did not light a lamp, although it was just a little after 10:00 p.m. But he was hungry enough to stoke up the fire.

He was surprised to find that Nora had left a pot of stew on the back of the stove. He made a full pot of coffee, and drank it with the stew.

Afterward, he threw the dregs of the coffee on the remains of the fire, putting it out. He rolled himself a smoke in darkness.

When he had finished, he ground it out and stepped to the door. Cloud haze had obscured the stars. The darkness was complete. Bill could see nothing in the darkness, nothing at all. It was dark as the inside of a coffin. It occurred to him that Cheyenne Robbins, besides being dangerous, might also be sly. He had given Bill until midnight. But he might copper his bet by arriving early. Apparently, if Shoemaker could be believed, Cheyenne was fighting for something besides driving Bill out of the country.

Bill stepped away from the door, avoiding the sounding board that the narrow porch made. His feet made a sucking sound in the soft mud of the yard. He held the shotgun across his chest and stepped carefully, trying to remember each thing that lay in the yard, and so to avoid stumbling.

Bill was not unused to danger. But always before, danger had been an impersonal thing, pitting itself against man and beast impartially and without fear or favor. This was vastly different. Bill could feel the empty churning in his stomach, the light-headedness, the trembling in his knees that fear could bring, the strangling tightness in his throat. He was a fool, he told himself. What chance had he against a gunfighter like Robbins? How did he know that Robbins would come alone? The very fact that Robbins had sought to cloak his grab with the pretense of driving Bill away lent belief to the notion that he would bring some of MC Bar's cowpunchers with him to ensure success.

Suddenly across the yard, he heard the slow, sliding sound of a horse. No. Two or three horses. He had not been mistaken. Cheyenne Robbins had not been content to rely on his gun speed, but on superiority in numbers and ruthlessness. He had to have the element of surprise with him as well. Bill's hands were trembling violently. He stood utterly still where he was and waited.

McCambridge's arrogant voice came harshly through the night: "He's gone. You did a job of putting the fear of God into him, Robbins."

Cheyenne's thin voice answered: "Guess I did." He laughed.

McCambridge said: "Let's go."

"No. I'm thinking we should be burning the shack first."

Bill Roebling spoke, knowing these words would probably be

his last: "No I don't think you will. Somehow I don't think you'll live long enough."

He could see nothing. But he could hear the small, fidgeting sounds the horses made. He knew that a fusillade of bullets would seek him out in another second. He fought the desire to move, to run, to fling himself down on his face. He held the double-barreled shotgun and waited. He wondered how many were there besides Cheyenne and McCambridge.

He had not long to wait. Cheyenne's gun blossomed brightly orange against the backdrop of night. The bullet tore into the mud at Bill's feet, showering him with a fine spray of mud. Cheyenne's gun fired again, but this time the bullet was ten feet to the right.

McCambridge opened up, and the horses moved closer to Bill. Suddenly all the tremors were gone from Bill's tight body. He raised the shotgun, waited a moment. Cheyenne's gun shouted again, and the bullet seared a long gash in Bill's thigh. But even after it had faded, the orange flash of Cheyenne's gun remained bright and plain in his eyes. Bill raised the gun and fired carefully, unerringly the left hand barrel.

A scream answered it. Now McCambridge and the two cowpunchers opened up in earnest. They had that shotgun flash to go by. A bullet tore through Bill's shoulder and whirled him around. He ran, not away from them, but just a way to one side. He had a nice target now and in the flares of their guns caught a glimpse of a riderless horse. He understood at last that the utter blackness of the night and the shotgun had almost evened the odds. A quick-draw man's talents are wasted in darkness. So is his unerring aim. So is almost anything except luck.

He stepped back until he judged that the buckshot from the remaining barrel would shower them all, and then he let it go. Howls greeted the gun's reverberating echoes. McCambridge's voice, lacking its bluster and arrogance, shouted: "Enough! Come on, let's get out of here! I tell ya, let's go!"

Bill was shoving two more shells into the shotgun's action. He closed the gun with a *snap*. The horses ran out of the yard, flinging gobs of the sticky mud into the air behind them. Far away along the road toward town, a woman screamed hollowly.

Nausea and dizziness soared through Bill Roebling's brain. He had downed one man. But he had no idea who it had been. It seemed too much to hope that it had been Robbins. That woman's scream could have come from none but Nora, returning. Returning to Bill Roebling, or returning to Cheyenne Robbins?

Carefully he took a step. The mud sucked noisily at his heavy boot. He took another. A slight sound before him made him stop. Now he could hear the running pound of the team, the frantic *screech* of the wagon wheels as Nora drove it recklessly into the yard. He lifted his voice and yelled: "Nora! Stay back! Don't come any closer!"

From the ground before him came that stirring again, the *click* of a hammer going back to full cock. Bill started to dive aside, knew with quick certainty that he was too late. Instead, then, he swung the shotgun muzzle toward the rustling noises on the ground. The revolver flared, and in that brief instant, Bill saw the muzzle of the shotgun directly beneath the flare. He pulled both triggers, firing not so much by sight as by instinct. Recoil drove him back. Recoil and the shock of Cheyenne's bullet that took a leg out from under him.

Things were hazy then for a while. Dimly he could hear Nora's frantic cries, and he tried to reply. There was something about this that he ought to be noticing, he knew. It escaped him for a while, and, when he realized what it was, he felt a deep and overpowering shame. Nora was not crying for Robbins. She was crying: "Bill! Bill! Where are you? Oh, darling, I was wrong!

I was wrong to desert you! Bill! Just be all right, and I'll never leave you again!"

He managed a one word croak—"Here."—and she was instantly beside him, her face wet from her weeping, her hands tender and soft.

He knew at last that his decision had been the right one, the only one he could have made. Even if he died. But he was not going to die. There was too much to live for now. He knew one other thing before the consciousness faded from him. Nora must never be allowed to realize that Bill was aware of Robbins's true purpose in trying to drive him away. She would feel enough responsibility for the scars he would carry without that, too. He raised a hand and pulled her face down against his, knowing now that he wasn't alone, had never been alone.

★ ★ ★ ★ ★

MONTANA GUNFIGHTER

★ ★ ★ ★ ★

I

They came down out of Montana in December of 1891. Early December. Roan Childress rode in the lead, Tolan behind. Their horses were gaunted with hunger, shaggy from the icy blasts of winter, and from their hoofs the shoes had long since worn away. Two men, answering a summons, accepting a job.

Roan was a big man in his mid twenties. Everything about Roan was big, his bones, his hands, his feet—big and hard from a lifetime of hard work. His hands, heavy-knuckled and broad, bore countless rope calluses on their palms. His eyes were the chill blue of a winter sky above a generous, straight nose. His mouth was wide, somber, yet it revealed the only softness apparent in the face. High cheek bones and hollow cheeks, now softly bearded with yellow whiskers, added to his gaunt appearance, as did the worn and trail-dirtied sheepskin that hung in loose folds from his thinned-out body. Roan's mouth could smile when his eyes did not. His mouth smiled now, ruefully, as he reined to a halt at the top of a long rise and stared down the twisting road into the main street of Antelope Junction. He hipped around in his saddle and said: "Hell of a sorry place to be at the end of a three-hundred-mile trail, ain't it?"

Earl Tolan nodded. He studied the town sourly for a moment, and then he asked in a voice cracked from disuse: "How's Houston goin' to contact us?"

"We register at the hotel. After that, it's up to him. He doesn't want to be seen talking to us, and he doesn't want us to show that we know him."

Tolan shrugged, and by mutual consent they touched heels to the sides of their horses and moved down the long, winding grade.

At the very edge of town, where the scrub sage ended and the weed-grown town lots began, Roan halted again. His face was bleak as he gazed down the ugly street lined with its unplanned collection of wind-blasted, false-fronted stores. Tolan pulled abreast of him and growled irritably: "What the hell you stopping for now?" Quite obviously he wanted to get on, was obviously savoring the prospect of liquor scalding down the length of his dry throat.

But Roan only kept staring somberly at the town, thinking that this was a dishonorable thing, but thinking, too, of his small outfit in northern Montana that he would lose altogether if he did not somehow obtain $600 by May 15th. That was mortgage-payment money. He said: "Last chance to back out, Earl. This is a dirty job ahead of us."

Tolan shook his head. "Uhn-uh. Last chance was back in Montana." His voice unconsciously took on a fiercely stubborn pride. "I gave my word to Houston then."

Childress smiled. "So you did. Your sacred word." There was faint bitterness in his voice.

Tolan looked at him without resentment. "A man needs something to live by." He stirred in his saddle impatiently. "We've put three hundred damned chilly miles behind us. Let's get in somewhere and get warm."

He nudged his horse, and they rode abreast down the wide and muddy street.

The mud was already hardening, in mid-afternoon, with night's coming cold. Light, fine snow drove along before the wind that whipped the horses' tails between their legs and stirred their long, shaggy hair. The street was almost deserted. A single man slogged along, head down, crossing the street ahead of them. A single horse was racked before the building that bore the painted legend *Custer Saloon* on its high front.

Roan murmured: "The battle of the Little Big Horn is still being fought." Beneath the sign hung a crudely painted scene of the battle, almost obscured now by the erosion of wind and time. He slid off his horse and wound the reins around the rail. He said: "One drink, Earl, and then these ponies get a feed."

There was sawdust on the saloon floor, and a pot-bellied stove red-hot between door and bar. A lone man stood at the bar, making idle, concentric rings in the moisture from the base of his beer glass. To the left of the bar and behind it, the dance floor stretched bare and dark and empty.

Roan grinned at the beer drinker companionably, fumbling at the buttons of his coat. "Quiet town. Where is everybody?" It got him a coldly suspicious stare. Roan shrugged and turned to the bartender, a balding, pale-faced man with gold-rimmed spectacles: "Whiskey. And what the hell's eating him?" He gestured with his head at the man with the beer.

The bartender slid out a couple of glasses and poured them full. He said in a flat and neutral tone: "Everybody's over at the courthouse. Otto Zulke's on trial for rustling."

"And?"

The man shrugged. "He'll be acquitted."

"You seem real sure."

"I'm sure enough. I'm sure of something else. When he is, there'll be hell to pay."

The lone man drained his beer and moved away from the bar, buttoning up his coat. He said disgustedly: "Everett, someday that mouth of yours will get you into trouble." He stalked through the front door, pulling his broad-brimmed hat down tightly upon his head as he disappeared.

Roan grinned and drained his glass. Tolan was watching the

bartender with his bright, alert eyes. Roan said: "Unsociable, ain't he?"

"Touchy," Everett said. "Everybody's touchy in this country. You passing through?"

Tolan started to speak, but Roan interrupted him. "We're looking for a place to winter. Hard times in Montana. No jobs."

The bartender examined him curiously for a moment, then turned his back without replying and began to polish glasses.

Roan laid $1 on the bar. He grinned at Tolan. "You look too damned comfortable to move. Stick around. I'll look after your horse."

Tolan's eyes were grateful. He downed his second drink and grunted: "Thanks. Maybe I will stay. You'll be back?"

"Uhn-huh. Pretty soon."

Roan shouldered through the door, wincing unconsciously at the bitter blast of wind. He untied both horses, and, holding the reins of Tolan's, he swung aboard his own. For an instant he sat there, a bit uncertain as his gaze roved up and down the street. Then, spotting the unmistakable huge bulk of a livery barn, he reined around.

Sensing what was in store for him, the horse broke into a trot, the led horse eagerly keeping abreast. Childress took a side street off Main, and, as he rounded the corner, he identified the courthouse, not only by its high, white-painted façade, but also by its bell cupola. He figured about thirty or forty saddle horses were tied before the building. And maybe fifteen or twenty wheel vehicles, ranging from heavy wagons to closed and curtained buggies the glory of whose black paint was not dimmed by the splashed coating of mud on their sides.

As Childress drew abreast of the courthouse, the low murmur of voices inside suddenly changed to a roar. Men spilled from the door, shouting, laughing, jeering, cursing. He reined up curiously. The crowd spilled down the steps onto the snow-covered lawn, and bunched there. A voice lifted: "Make way! Make way!"

A girl came from the courthouse door. Roan stared at her dumbly. He couldn't distinguish her features at such a distance, but her body eloquently revealed her state of mind. She took a defiant stance at the top of the steps, and every inch of her proclaimed her indignation. The same voice yelled: "Let the lady through!"

Roan could see the flush that stained the girl's face. Her hair was a deep shade of copper and even on this sunless day it threw off gleaming highlights. Her full, high breasts heaved with her rapid breathing. Roan felt a stir of admiration, reminded at once of a wild mare, caught, and trembling with defiance at the restraint. He hardly recalled dismounting. He only knew he had to have a closer look at this girl. He had to know if her face fulfilled the promise of her body.

The crowd surrounded the girl, blocking the courthouse door. In it, Roan could hear a voice he recognized, a curt, commanding, military voice that could only belong to Colonel Simon Houston. "Orr! Coates! Clear this damned rabble away from the door!"

Childress smiled, but he kept moving, shouldering his way through the milling crowd. The girl still stood at the top of the steps, but now she was hemmed in, crowded from all sides. Her face had paled, drawn taut by something close to panic. Childress could feel the ugly hostility of the crowd. The girl tried to make her way back to the courthouse door, but it was like bucking the raging current of a mountain stream. At last, with slumping shoulders, she gave it up.

Childress could see her face as she turned back. Wide and frightened, her eyes stared out over the heads of the crowd, stared out and found his own. Then Childress put all of his weight and strength into fighting that crowd. Foot by foot he neared the steps. Back inside the courthouse, Houston's voice assumed a petulant frustration as he kept calling for someone named Orr, and for another named Coates.

Childress reached the foot of the steps. All around, men were cursing him, but he retained the even gravity of his expression, until he heard the girl scream, heard the scream choked off. He slammed half a dozen men roughly from his path. He saw the girl in the tight grasp of a bearded, burly, tobacco-stained man who shouted in a voice heavy with laughter: "I'll get you to your buggy, Janet, but, by damn, it'll cost you a kiss!"

The girl fought, twisting her head from side to side. Inexorably the bearded lips came down close to her face. Suddenly her teeth flashed white and sank into the man's bearded cheek. With a howl of pain, he flung her away from him. His heavy hand came up, rang loudly as it slapped her cheek. Her head rocked with the force of the blow.

Childress gained the top of the steps at last. He put out a big hand and spun the bearded man around. Wordlessly he swung with a stiff left and saw the man's head snap back. He followed with a right that landed flushly in the man's mouth. He felt lips and teeth give before his knuckles.

There was some approval in the crowd for this, but there was also the slow stirring of anger and resentment. Even as he fought, Childress could tell that. He judged that the approval arose because most of them respected this girl. The anger and resentment, he did not yet understand.

The bearded man, thrown back at him by the press of bodies into which he had fallen, landed a punch on Roan's forehead. The force of it put a brackish taste in his mouth and made his head whirl. Wildness drove that whirling from his brain. Wildness took him as it always did, and he lunged at the bearded man, his fists driving out with the hardness and force of sledges driving a stake. The big man could not go down. Roan's punches could not put him down, for the bodies into which he fell supported him.

He put his hands up in a futile attempt to defend himself from Roan, and Roan lowered his hands and drove blows to the man's belly, blows that made the wind sigh out of him as it might from a bellows. He lowered his hands to protect his belly, and Roan brought one up from waist level. It landed flushly on the point of the man's jaw. The bearded one fell then, his knees buckling under him as though made of gelatin.

Roan turned back to the girl, only to find a tall, hollow-cheeked man holding a cocked Colt .44 trained on his midsection. Roan grinned tightly and stooped to retrieve his hat. Temper took him over fast and he lunged in under the tall man's gun hand, forcing it upward with his rising body. Then, hat forgotten, he brought a knee into the tall man's groin.

The .44 racketed at the sky. Childress straightened, got the gun wrist in his two big hands, and twisted savagely. The tall man made a high, thin sound of pain, and the .44 fell onto the courthouse steps. Childress kept twisting that arm, whirled the tall man around until the arm was high against his shoulder blades. He said in a soft, flat voice: "Next time you pull a gun, I'd advise you to shoot it. Because next time I'll break your arm."

The man's voice, hissing out from between pain-clenched teeth, was as fraught with menace as the chatter of a prairie rattlesnake. "I will," he said. "You can count on it."

Roan heard another voice now, over the quiet that had suddenly taken the crowd. "Here, here . . . what's going on?" Roan swung his head. He saw the silver star first, and after that, the seamed, leathery face above it. He saw the white cavalry mustache, startling against the dark mahogany skin, and the eyes, blue and perhaps a little bewildered. The sheriff said: "Stop it now. Let him go."

49

Roan released his man, who whirled and put his deadly, pale yellow eyes on Childress's face.

Colonel Houston came from behind the sheriff, a stocky, paunchy, pompous man, reminding Roan of bantam rooster at this moment. The colonel turned to a round-faced, florid man beside him and asked petulantly: "Guthrie, what's going on?" Without waiting for a reply, he turned back toward Coates, and now his voice held confident authority: "Ranse, what's going on? What's going on? Let's get out of here."

Ransom Coates's eyes were instantly hooded. He inclined his head respectfully at Houston, but, as he passed Roan on the way down the steps, he said softly: "Some other time, bucko. Some other time."

And then he was gone, driving a wedge through the crowd, a wedge that carried Houston, the girl, Guthrie, and the sheriff along with him. Men fell away uneasily before this cadaverous man with the pale eyes, and the fear Roan saw in their faces made him angry and ashamed in their behalf. He retrieved his hat and eased himself out of the hostile crowd. If he had listened, their muttered comments might have warned him. But he did not listen. For he was thinking of a girl, of a girl with gleaming copper hair, one who for a moment had reminded him of a wild mare, caught and trembling at the restraint.

II

The crowd built knots as it scattered, knots of talking, excited men. One element pushed on through as the colonel, his daughter, and Ransom Coates had done, and this element came under the hard, hostile scrutiny of those who remained. For the most part, these men drove away in buggies and buckboards. A few mounted saddle horses. After they had gone, however, the only vehicles left were the heavy wagons.

It took no particular astuteness to separate the crowd into

factions. Childress knew that those who had gone were the syndicate men, the big ranchers, while those who remained were the settlers and the small ranchers. He caught the two horses and mounted his own, holding the reins of Tolan's. Attention shifted from him as he sat there, shifted to a man who had just come out of the courthouse. The crowd's murmur deepened, and a voice shouted: "We showed 'em, Otto! We showed 'em, boy!"

He noticed the big, bearded man he had knocked down, in the crowd surrounding Otto Zulke, and then he rode away in the direction of the stable.

Riding, he told himself wryly: *You've done all right for a starter. You've made an enemy on the side of the settlers and another on the syndicate's side. And you've made no friends.* Remembering Ransom Coates's low-voiced promise, he felt a stir of uneasiness. But suddenly he brightened. Except for Coates's intervention, he would have been finished here even before he began. For the settlers would never have accepted into their ranks one who had whipped a member of their group for annoying the colonel's daughter. Coates had changed that. Smiling, Roan dismounted before the stable and led his horses inside.

When he came out, it was snowing in earnest. Overhead, the clouds had darkened, and here and there he passed a lamplit window although it was not yet 4:00 p.m. The wind was colder, too. Roan judged the temperature to be somewhere near the zero mark.

He lowered his head and bucked the wind, heading back toward the Custer Saloon. As he passed the courthouse, a man detached himself from the shadows on the porch and came down the steps. Roan's muscles tightened involuntarily, but he did not slow his pace. The man called: "Wait a minute, stranger! I'll walk along with you."

Roan stopped, wary and alert. The man neared him and stuck

out a hand that was red with cold. "I'm Philo Manette," he said, his voice deep and humorous.

"Roan Childress." He took the hand. There was strength in Manette's grasp, but Roan recognized it as only a friendly pressure, completely lacking in that domineering, crushing strength so often found in a first handshake. Roan liked Manette immediately. He asked: "Which side of this ruckus are you on?"

Manette laughed. He was about as tall as Roan, but there was a good deal more solidity to him. He wore a short, black beard, and his nose above it was almost Grecian in its classic beauty. His eyes were dark and held considerable softness and good humor. He countered: "Do I look like a syndicate man?"

Roan grinned. "Hardly."

Manette wore a ragged, voluminous sheepskin and his wide-brimmed black hat was shapeless with age and hard usage. His boots were scuffed and muddy below clean, faded Levi's. Manette matched Roan's hurrying pace. "I'd like to buy you a drink," he said.

"I'm headed for the Custer Saloon. I left my friend there while I put up the horses."

"Good. The Custer, then." He walked in silence a few moments, then asked in a voice that had its teasing undertone: "Do you always manage to get involved in two fights the first day you hit a new town?"

"Not always." Roan's liking for Manette kept growing. He discovered that he was smiling.

Manette murmured: "You couldn't have picked worse men to quarrel with. I hope you know that."

Roan said nothing.

"I kind of liked the way you handled yourself," Manette said. "I guess I figured you had earned a warning. The big, bearded man you knocked down is Lyle Weeks. He's got a place about five miles from mine. He's a man with pride, Childress. He'll not forget the way you roughed him up."

Roan shrugged.

Manette went on: "But he's nothing compared to the other one. Coates is a killer, a bad one. So watch them both, my friend. Watch them both because they'll both be watching you." They reached the Custer, and Manette pushed open the door. The warmth of the room enveloped them as they stepped inside. Manette yelled at the boisterous crowd: "Boys, this is Roan Childress, the man that took Ranse's gun away from him. He may not be with us long, but treat him right while he is."

Manette's sally drew a guffaw of laughter from the crowd. Roan felt himself flushing. He didn't miss the implications of Manette's grim humor. They surrounded him, pounded him on back and shoulders with hearty hands. He felt like a Judas. For these were the men he had come to betray. The mood of the crowd was jubilant. Yet under its surface there ran a current of uneasiness that Childress could sense but could not understand.

Tolan was getting drunk as rapidly as he could, and already his eyes had the peculiar, glazed look they assumed whenever he took more than two or three drinks. He gave one of his thin-lipped, brief grins as Roan stepped up beside him. Manette stepped up on the other side of Tolan, and Childress said: "Earl, meet Philo Manette."

Tolan shook hands gravely with Manette, studying him owl-ishly. Talk buzzed around them briefly, then stopped as another man came into the saloon.

Roan instantly recognized him as Otto Zulke, the rustler who had been on trial. He was a short man, and an incredibly broad one. Though less than five feet six, he must have weighed a full two hundred pounds. His legs were short and slightly bowed, his chest a veritable barrel. He thumbed back his hat, revealing his baldness, and his face wreathed itself into a cheerful grin. He shouted: "Boys, we showed 'em! Maybe they've got the state government in their hip pockets, but they ain't got Corbin County!"

Manette muttered audibly: "You damn' fool."

Roan turned, his expression questioning. Manette became cautious, and then what he saw in Roan's face reassured him. He said: "The court acquitted Zulke, but he's a fool if he thinks it's finished. It ain't. Not by a whole lot."

"How's that?"

"Why the colonel got up right after the jury handed in their verdict. Made quite a speech. The jist of it was that, if the courts in Corbin County couldn't convict a known rustler that was caught with the goods, then it was time some things got changed. He made it pretty plain that in the future the big outfits would try to convict their own rustlers."

Childless felt a flash of anxiety that he tried to conceal. He said: "Was Zulke caught with the goods?"

Manette nodded. Again it was plain that he thought he was talking too much.

Roan might have pursued the subject further, but Earl lowered his head, pillowing it briefly and tiredly on the bar. Roan touched his arm. "Let's get something to eat," he said, "and find us a bed. It's been a long day."

Surprisingly Tolan did not object. He followed meekly as Roan shouldered his way through the crowd and out into the bitter, snow-laden wind.

III

Janet Houston wondered at the small-girl guilt that plagued her as she got into the buggy. She sat quietly while the colonel, her father, arranged the heavy buffalo robe over her knees. She felt just as she often had in childhood, awaiting chastisement for some naughtiness. Her father's face was cold and grim, and his lips showed an anger that he obviously found hard to control.

He climbed up beside her and slapped the buggy horse's back with the reins. The vehicle moved downstreet toward the hotel. Janet studied him uneasily from the corner of her eye.

She saw a man of fifty or so, his hat shoved back on his balding forehead, a liberal sprinkling of gray in the red hair at his temples. His complexion was florid from a lifetime spent out-of-doors, and veins made a red tracery about his bulbous nose and puffy cheeks. His neck was a bull's neck, solid and muscular, rising but slightly out of his ponderous shoulders. He held his back ramrod straight, as always, for Houston's vanity was his military bearing and demeanor. A hard man, Colonel Houston. Janet had never seen him show tenderness for a single living thing save herself.

She knew a little of his military history. He'd ridden with Slough and the 1st Colorado Volunteers in the battle of Apache Cañon and in the battle of Pigeon's Ranche. He'd formed an attachment to Colonel Chivington, and had served under him afterward in the so-called Battle of Sand Creek, which in reality was a brutal and savage massacre. He had not shared Chivington's disgrace over that affair, but had gone on to distinguish himself in later Indian battles. In a curtailed frontier Army, he had never passed the rank of lieutenant. The rank of colonel, by which he now went, he owed to the earlier years with the Volunteers before he joined the Regular Army. He was a man with little pity, with no understanding of weakness, a man to whom softness was weakness, to whom tenderness was maudlin.

"We'll stay in town tonight," Houston said shortly. "It's too late to drive home now."

Janet said nothing. After a moment's silence, Houston turned and put his bright-eyed, searching stare upon her. "What was the trouble on the courthouse porch?"

"A fight. It was nothing, Father." She wondered at her reluctance to give him the facts.

"What was the fight about?"

"I don't know," she lied. "I guess it wasn't important."

Houston drew back on the reins and the buggy stopped. His voice, though quiet, nevertheless made its implacable demand: "What was the fight about?"

Janet knew this tone and feared him when he used it. She could feel the blood leaving her face. She gulped, trying to think up some reasonable fairy tale, but Houston said in the same inflexible tone: "There is no use in trying to conceal it from me. I'll find out whether you tell me or not."

Janet shrugged resignedly. "Lyle Weeks roughed me up. I was hemmed in by the crowd. He grabbed me and said he'd see me to the buggy."

The buggy horse fidgeted and pranced, but Houston held him still with savagely tightened reins. The animal backed. "The fight, girl. The fight."

"I'm coming to that." Now she could feel her face grow hot. "He demanded a kiss for seeing me to the buggy. I fought him." She laughed nervously. "I bit his cheek, and he hit me. Then they were fighting, Weeks and some stranger. The stranger knocked him down, and then Ransom got through the crowd. Maybe he didn't quite understand, because he pulled his gun on the stranger." Janet smiled then. "The stranger took his gun away from him. You can imagine how that affected Ransom."

But Houston did not seem to be thinking of the stranger, or of Ransom Coates. He clucked to the buggy horse, his eyes as cold as the howling zero wind. He muttered: "Weeks, huh? Damn them, they're getting brave now . . . and foolish."

Janet shivered, touched by an inner chill. "Forget it Father. I wasn't hurt."

He pulled the buggy to a halt before the hotel. Coates immediately appeared at its side, reaching up a proprietary hand for Janet. Faintly irritated, she took it and climbed down to the walk. Houston got down pompously and strutted behind her into the hotel lobby. He said curtly: "Go on up. I'll join you later."

"All right, Father." But at the stairway she turned. She saw her father and Coates heading into the bar. The colonel was talking angrily, his face red, and Janet knew he was talking about Weeks.

Lifting her skirts, she climbed the stairs. Suddenly she was afraid. Someway, somehow, she sensed that sinister forces were at work. She had thought she knew her father, but now, considering it, she wondered if she really did. There had been a certain implacable coldness in the colonel tonight, an unfamiliar quiet anger, whose very quietness made it all the more terrifying.

She opened the door to their suite, which included a small sitting room and two smaller bedrooms. A pot-bellied, cast-iron stove sat in the center of the sitting room, surrounded by well-worn furniture.

Janet shrugged out of her heavy buffalo coat and laid it over the back of a chair. She was a small girl, yet she invested her every movement with a lithe, animal-like quality. More than soft flesh lurked beneath the rustling silk of Janet's gown. She owned smooth, sinuous muscles, and she was made as a woman should be, with wide, full hips, firm, high-thrusting breasts, and a tiny waist. Her face, with its high cheek bones, faintly hollow cheeks, and lightly olive complexion betrayed a Creole origin, but that copper hair was a direct legacy from the colonel—as was her temper. She remembered the way her temper had flared at Weeks, recalled with a flush of shame the way she had bitten him. But suddenly she began to smile. *I'll bet he'll think twice before he lays his hands on me again,* she mused with considerable pleasure.

She backed close to the stove, spreading her hands to its

welcome warmth, and abruptly she was glad that her father had decided to spend the night in town. Now she remembered the stranger, and the corners of her full red mouth lifted in a more sensuous smile. Tall, he had been, tall and wearing a week's growth of yellow whiskers. She tried to recall the shade of his eyes and decided they must have been blue. A man you remembered. A man shaped by the saddle, by rope and gun, formed by the merciless beat of sun heat in summer, carved by the icy blasts of winter. She compared him with Ransom Coates, and, perhaps because she resented the proprietary assurance which Coates put into his matter-of-fact courtship, she stopped comparing them and thought only of the stranger. Her smile grew pensive, and her eyes turned very soft.

Coming up here, she had intended to undress, knowing that the colonel would have supper sent up later. But now she changed her mind. Instead of undressing, she went over to the mirror and began to brush her hair.

A cold draft came from the window. Flakes of snow sifted in between its frame and the warped sill. Janet felt a vast loneliness, a need for tenderness and companionship. She thought: *Father used to talk to me and I miss it. He's been different since this rustling business came up.* She was remembering herself as she had been as a small girl, tucked in between clean, cool sheets at night and begging for a story while her pudgy hands tugged at her beribboned pigtails. She was remembering the stories he had told, of the charge of the Colorado Cavalry at Apache Cañon, the savage brutality of the Sand Creek story. Hardly tales for a small girl, but he told them with an excited exuberance that held her enthralled.

"Six hundred of them, men, women, kids. They were camped in a valley, a kind of ravine. We came sweeping down on them from the tops of both ridges in a foot of snow. Took 'em completely by surprise. I can see Chivington yet, a big, soldierly man on a black horse. He yelled . . . 'No quarter and no prisoners! Charge!' "

Chilling suddenly, Janet got up and went to the stove. She stood very close to it. Slowly her chill abated. Yet, even with the chill gone, Janet Houston was afraid.

IV

There was a restaurant with dirty, steamed-up windows a couple of doors from the hotel, but Roan only gave it brief attention. Tonight, he wanted a good meal to make up for all the bad ones along the trail. Also he wanted to sign his name on the hotel register so the colonel would find it there when he checked it over. Roan caught himself thinking of other comforts, of a bath and a shave and a night in a soft hotel bed.

The lobby turned out to be a rather large, high-ceilinged room with a white tile floor. Between door and desk ran a four-foot-wide carpet runner of a deep rose color, worn and now tracked with mud. Leather-covered settees were scattered along the walls beneath game heads ranging from antelope to cougar, from moose to jack rabbits.

Tolan staggered slightly as he followed Roan to the desk. The clerk, a balding, elderly man with spectacles shoved low on his nose so that he could peer over them, flipped open the register and shoved it at them.

They signed. The clerk said—"That'll be a dollar, gents . . ."— and added, eyeing them carefully: "in advance."

Roan forked over a dollar. He said: "Barbershop?"

"Next door. You can get to it through the hotel bar."

Childress looked at Tolan. "Coming,"

Tolan shook his head. His eyes were still glazed. "I'll take a snooze first."

Roan watched Tolan climb the stairs, but his sympathy changed to curiosity as he saw a woman's trim ankles and lifted skirt pass Tolan, coming down.

Janet Houston reached the landing and came down the last four steps. She came to Roan at once and there was neither hesitation nor shyness in her manner as she said: "I've been hoping I'd see you. I wanted to thank you for what you did for me this afternoon."

Her eyes, Roan saw now, were a deep, soft brown. And in this combination of lamplight and cold dusk light her dark copper hair showed glints that were almost metallic. Roan grinned down at her. "You were doing all right without me."

She flushed and lowered her glance. "I wasn't very lady-like, was I?"

Roan felt a compulsion to defend her. "I'd say you did just right."

She looked up at him then, warmly grateful. "You're a stranger in Antelope Junction, aren't you? Will you be staying here?"

"Depends," he said, "on whether there is work to be had."

"I'll speak to my father."

He said—"No."—but did not explain why.

Janet studied him intently for a moment. "Because of Ransom Coates?"

"Maybe. Maybe I just like to get my own jobs."

He heard the colonel's harsh bark from across the lobby at the bar entrance: "Janet!"

She said softly: "Excuse me." Roan saw anger in her eyes as she turned, but he did not know whether it was directed at him for his independent attitude, or at the colonel for his peremptory tone.

He lounged on the counter and watched as they crossed the lobby and entered the dining room. Then he turned and headed through the bar toward the barbershop door at its far end.

Coates stood at one end of the bar, an untouched drink

before him. He regarded Roan with dully smoldering eyes, but he did not speak, and he did not move.

Both barbershop chairs were filled, and Roan found a waiting line on the long bench against the wall. Clouds of steam rolled out of the back room, accompanied by ribald laughter and coarse jests, and on another bench near this door a second line of customers awaited their turns at the oaken tubs.

Roan sat down in a vacant space at the near end of the bath bench and fished his sack of Durham from his pocket. A man in one of the barber chairs was holding forth on the country's big man/little man controversy. "Damn 'em," he said, "we got 'em runnin' now. They know no Corbin County jury will convict a man of rustlin' on their say so."

Childress finished rolling his cigarette, licked the paper, and wiped a match alight on the underside of the bench. A man next to him said loudly: "Don't get too cocky, Russ. Don't get too cocky. Judge Pumphrey says they kin git what he calls a change of venue. That means they kin git rustlers tried in some other county."

The man in the chair laughed scornfully. "Then why didn't they do that with Otto?" He put his bright glance on the man who had spoken, and then his eyes flicked to Roan and widened. A grin spread out across his freckled face. "Hey," he said, "ain't you the fella that took Ranse's gun away from him?"

Roan nodded, embarrassed by the sudden attention he was getting. He knew why he had not been recognized sooner. He looked different without his sheepskin and hat, which he had taken off before entering. And he noticed a sudden stiffening about the man in the other barber chair, whose back was toward him. Studying the man's broad back, he decided that this was the one he had knocked down for molesting Janet Houston.

Russ said slyly: "An' you roughed up Lyle here."

Weeks came up out of the barber chair and whirled, glowering. He blustered: "Took me by surprise, the son-of-a-bitch!"

Childress stood up. "Want to finish it now?" he asked.

A new voice broke into the tense silence that followed: "Hey, hey, cut it out!"

This was Manette, lounging just inside the door between hotel bar and barbershop. He said: "Lyle, damn it, you had a lickin' coming this afternoon. If Childress hadn't done it, I would. Now let him alone. I need a man out home, and I don't want one so damned beat up he can't work."

Weeks growled something unintelligible, and crawled gratefully back into the barber chair. His relief at thus being afforded a chance to save both his pride and himself from another go with Roan was very plain and drew more than one smile from the waiting crowd. Roan sat down, and Manette sank down beside him.

Manette said: "You know you're the fair-haired boy around here, don't you?"

"What for?"

"For taking Ranse's gun away from him."

The subject embarrassed Roan so he muttered: "You said something about needing a man. That on the level?"

"Sure is. You want a job? This is a damned poor country for a man to stop in, though, I'll tell you that."

"I'm tired of traveling," Roan said. "A job sounds good. How about Tolan?"

"I'll use him, too." But Manette was less enthusiastic about this.

Roan grinned. "You got yourself a pair of men. How big a place you got?"

"Hundred and sixty. Best water in Corbin County. And all of Wyoming around it."

"There's a catch," Roan said. "A hundred and sixty won't support two hired hands."

Manette grinned. "Sure there's a catch. Houston claims everything right up to my fence line."

Roan said: "Gun job then?"

"Call it that if you want. I told you I liked the way you handled yourself."

"I'll let you know tomorrow. I'll have to talk to Earl."

"Sure. Take all the time you want. When you decide, ride out." Manette got up, but he looked down at Roan seriously for a moment, as though trying to satisfy himself that his earlier judgment of Roan was correct.

Roan found difficulty in meeting his eyes until he thought: *Hell, they're all either rustling or condoning it in others. They've got things fixed so the outfits they're stealing from can't do a damned thing about it.* After that, his eyes bored steadily into Manette's.

The big man turned away with a final grin and a squeeze of Roan's shoulder. He went through the outside door into the howling wind, leaving Roan Childress to take stock of himself.

Roan Childress had been raised in the saddle. Orphaned at ten, and big for his age, he'd got a job with an outfit near Butte as chore boy, but by the time he was twelve, he was riding with the crew. He made a deal with the boss when he was fourteen, a deal whereby he could buy a few head of cattle and run them with the boss stock. And at twenty, he shipped fifty steers, bought a little place of his own, and quit his job. So he had a true cowman's hatred of rustling. In fact, he owed his present difficulty to the fact that rustlers had included twenty-five head of his stock in a larger bunch rustled from his neighbors. He'd been counting on those steers to make his mortgage payments. They'd been grazing a lush piece of range nearly ten miles from the home place, fattening up for the drive to the railroad. But when he'd gone after them, he found them missing. Long enough gone so that there were no tracks to follow. . . .

His turn came at the baths, and he went into the back room

and stripped off his clothes. Except for his hands, wrists, neck, and face, his body was white, but corded with long ropy muscles that bunched and tightened with each small movement. He squeezed himself into one of the small, oaken tubs, and soaked gratefully in the steaming water. He stood up, lathered thoroughly, and then splashed rinse water over himself.

He dressed thoughtfully, went out, and got into a vacant barber chair.

Almost all of the crowd had left. Roan lay back while the barber lathered his face and began to shave him. His body relaxed, but his mind did not. Somewhere down deep guilt stirred, thoroughly angering him, making him argue with too much heat: *A rustler's a rustler wherever you find him and however much you happen to like him. And I'm getting paid for collecting the evidence Houston needs to convict.* But still, doubt put a frown upon his broad forehead.

V

Ransom Coates stood at the bar in such a position that he could see through the glass door panel into the barbershop. He saw Lyle Weeks come out and take a position at the far end of the bar. He stared at Weeks with smoldering eyes. Later, he saw Roan Childress take an empty barber chair, and transferred his gaze from Weeks to Roan.

Being disarmed before so large a group of settlers had rubbed Coates's pride raw. He'd be able to get even with Weeks for manhandling Janet, but he wished there were some way of getting even with Roan. Colonel Houston had given him a job to do on Weeks, one he would enjoy. Weeks was to be pistol-whipped. The colonel wanted a thorough job in order, as he put it, to "teach the damned rabble some manners toward their betters." But that still left Childress.

So, waiting for Weeks to leave, Coates brooded about Childress and the score he had to settle with him. Suddenly an idea came to him and his long hollow face softened with satisfaction. Hell, there was a way to do this, and the colonel need be none the wiser. He could simply say. . . .

He grinned and tossed his drink down. He studied Weeks carefully, trying to gauge the man's thoughts and intentions. He guessed, from the animated conversation Weeks was having with the man next to him, that the settler would be at the bar a while longer. Maybe long enough.

Coates left the bar, crossed the hotel lobby, and went out into the wind. Although it was not much after 6:00 p.m., full dark had come quickly over the land. The wind was a solid, tangible thing blowing with such steady pressure out of the north. It howled around the eaves of the buildings and it kept the air full to saturation with blowing snow.

Coates gathered his short sheepskin around him, belting it securely at the waist. He turned up the collar and partially buried his face in its warmth. Then, head down and hat pulled tightly on his head, he hurried along the street.

He passed the Custer without a glance, and passed a couple of other, smaller saloons. He came at last to one called the Ace High, and here he left the walk and took to the bare vacant lot beside it. He came up in the rear and, without knocking, opened the back door.

A boy sat up on a cot against the wall, looked at him, and reached for a match to light the lamp that sat on a box beside his bed.

Coates said quickly: "Never mind, Manuel. It's me, Ranse Coates. You want to make a dollar tonight?"

"*Sí. Bueno, señor.*"

The boy put on his pants and slipped his feet into a pair of down-at-the-heel shoes that were overly large for him. He reached for a ragged coat, also a hand-me-down that hung from a nail on the wall.

"The colonel wants to see a man," Coates said, "but he doesn't want anyone to know about it. You've done this kind of thing before so you know enough to keep your mouth shut about it."

"Who is the man, *señor*, and where does the colonel wish to see him?"

Coates handed the boy a dollar. "He's a tall, yellow-haired man and he's staying at the hotel. The colonel wants to see him down at the Capitan Livery Barn. Don't let anyone overhear what you say to him. His name is Roan Childress."

Without waiting for the boy's reply, he turned and went back out into the alley. Hurrying now, he returned to the hotel and took his place at the bar. Weeks was still listening to the man next to him but his increasing restlessness told Coates that he wanted to break away.

Coates ordered a drink and tossed it down quickly. Weeks said good bye to his companion and turned. He walked past Coates, studiously avoided glancing at him, and went out through the lobby to the front door. He had the appearance of a man heading home. Coates followed him.

Weeks headed toward the Custer, head down, oblivious to everything but the storm. Coates untied his horse from the rail in front of the hotel, brushed snow from his saddle, and swung into it.

He passed his quarry at a brisk trot, turned his head, and saw Weeks pause before the Custer, staring at its doors. But Weeks did not go in. With hands already apparently stiff from cold, he untied his reins and swung to his saddle.

Coates held his own reins in his left hand and shoved the right deep into the pocket of his sheepskin. He dug spurs into his horse's ribs and rode south at a gallop, hoof beats muffled by deepening snow.

A mile from town the road crossed Rustler Creek by a wooden bridge. Here Coates reined up, swinging his horse to face the north.

He waited, keeping his right hand warm in his pocket. Once, he withdrew it long enough to lift the skirt of his coat above his holstered gun. Then he returned the hand to the pocket and kept flexing it as the seconds ticked away. A certain tension came to him, but it was a pleasant thing—the hunter's waiting excitement, the stimulant that turns the killer wolf's eyes bright as he stalks his kill.

He heard Weeks's softly cursing voice carried on the bitter, howling wind. He heard Weeks coming, and at last saw his hunched-over shape against the background of swirling white.

Coates waited until Weeks was almost upon him, and then he called: "Weeks! The colonel sent me to tell you he won't stand for a stinking settler's hands on Miss Janet!"

Weeks straightened convulsively and clawed for his gun. His coat impeded his hands, but Coates had no such handicap. His gun came up smoothly, belched once, and was silent.

The sound of murder drifted away on the shrieking wind. Weeks's horse whistled shrilly, reared, and dumped Weeks's inert body from the saddle. Then it galloped away into the storm.

Coates smiled as he returned his gun to its holster. Without a second glance at the body on the ground, he rode along the road in the direction of town. The killing had stimulated him. He felt powerful, strong, alight. The cold no longer bothered him, for his blood was racing quickly through his gaunt body.

He rode into town and put his horse up at the Drover's Livery Barn. After that, he strode, head down, toward the hotel to report to Colonel Houston. Confidently he rehearsed his story. "Hell," he'd say, "I hardly spoke to the fool and he grabbed for his iron. I didn't have no choice."

Good. The way he'd rigged it beforehand, he hadn't had any

choice. And those damned settlers wouldn't have any choice, either. They'd be bound to figure Childress beefed Weeks, and they'd run him out of the country.

VI

At 8:00 p.m., Roan Childress was chilled to the bone and thoroughly angry. He had answered the ragged Mexican boy's summons almost immediately, and had been waiting ever since in the dismal, cold depths of the deserted Capitan Livery Barn.

Stamping his feet, shivering in spite of himself, he cursed bitterly and made his way out into the street. "You damn' fool," he said aloud. Fool for waiting nearly two hours here in the cold. Fool for coming to Antelope Junction in the first place. Fool.

Then he thought of Janet Houston and knew he regretted none of it. He thought of her serene self-possession, of her lack of the coy artificiality he had found in so many other women. Janet was as direct as a child and apparently as uncomplicated. She was all woman, with those clear brown eyes, full, soft lips, and flaming copper hair. Yet she was not for him, a range detective hired by her father to collect evidence of rustling against the settlers and small cowmen. She was so used to rich living, she would think of his Montana spread as a squatter's claim, and consider his tight log house little better than a sod hogan. She was not for him, and the realization made his eyes turn empty and cold.

He saw the sheriff lounging in the hotel lobby as he went in, stamping snow from his boots, brushing it from his coat. He noticed the cold-eyed inspection he got from the sheriff. In an irritable frame of mind, he clumped up the stairs to his room.

The room was dark. He struck a match, raised the lamp chimney, and touched the flame to the wick. Earl Tolan lay on the bed, awake, watching him inscrutably.

"You damn' fool," Tolan said.

Roan frowned. "What the hell's eating you?"

Tolan's voice was sarcastic. "You don't know, I suppose."

"No, I don't."

"Well, maybe you know this. They found his body."

"What the hell are you talking about? Whose body?"

"Weeks. Lyle Weeks. The one you roughed up for manhandling Houston's daughter."

"He's dead?"

"Deader'n hell. Shot in the heart. There's only one thing in your favor, an' that is he had his gun in his hand, an' was shot from the front. The sheriff was just up here looking for you."

"He thinks I did it? Why?"

"You had a ruckus with Weeks at the courthouse, another later in the barbershop. You've been gone for a couple of hours, ever since you got through in the barbershop."

"Houston sent for me."

"You talked to him then?"

Roan shook his head. "I was supposed to go to the Capitan Livery Stable. But there wasn't anyone there. I finally got sick of waiting."

Tolan sat up on the bed. He gave Roan his close scrutiny for a moment, then yawned and stretched. "Somebody's trying to hang a frame around you. Well, hell, tell 'em Weeks drawed on you an' you beat him to it."

"To hell with that. I didn't kill him."

Tolan's thin face expressed disgust. "So what will you tell them? That Houston sent for you and that you've been waiting over at the Capitan for him to show up? That'd fix us good."

Roan frowned. "I'm going to see the colonel," he said.

Tolan muttered: "End of the hall on the right. I saw the girl go in a while ago."

Roan opened the door and peered into the hall. It was deserted, but he heard a man's voice rising from the lobby.

"Sheriff, what the hell's holdin' you back? Go get him."

And the sheriff's protest: "Maybe it was self-defense. Looked like it, you got to admit. But I'll go on up."

Roan hurried down the hall and knocked on Houston's door. The door opened and Houston stood facing him, short, portly, imperious. "What do you want?"

"I'm Roan Childress. You've sure got a short memory." He stepped into the room and pushed the door shut behind him. He said: "You had Weeks killed, didn't you? You sent me a phony message by that Mexican kid so I wouldn't be able to explain where I was when he was killed."

"I don't know what you're talking about."

"I think you do."

"I didn't send you any message." The colonel seemed irritated and defensive, yet Roan got the odd impression that the man was telling the truth. He said: "Apparently there's only one way out of it for me. And that's to admit the killing and claim self-defense. But I didn't do it and I want that known, at least by you."

Houston growled: "You're no damned good to me if you admit killing Weeks. He's one of them, and they'll have no truck with you after you admit killing him."

Roan smiled coldly. "You're wrong there, mister. I've already got an offer of a job at Philo Manette's."

The name seemed to work magic on the colonel. A surface geniality relaxed his rigid stance and softened the mold of his broad, harsh countenance. He said: "You're a reckless man, Childress. You've been in Antelope Junction less than half a day, yet you've stirred up more trouble in that time than most men do in a year. All right. Have at it. Admit the killing and take your job with Manette. You know who he is, of course?"

"No. Is he someone special?"

"He's the ringleader of the settler faction. And I want him

70

most of all."

"All right," Roan said. "If he's a rustler, you'll get him." He stared at the colonel for a moment, gauging him, and out of that appraisal came his next demand: "I'll take the six hundred that was promised me before I ride out to Manette's. And the first month's pay due Tolan."

His deal with Houston, made a month ago in Montana, had specified that payment in advance so he could send it back to pay off his mortgage.

The colonel flushed slightly, but he did not hesitate. He went to a desk and took a canvas bag from its drawer. Then, counting out heavy double eagles, he flung them down one by one upon its top. Thirty. Thirty times the golden coins rang on the desk. There was a parallel in that, an unpleasant one that Roan's mind recognized and rejected. The colonel finished counting Roan's advance and laid out Tolan's beside it. Roan scooped the coins into his hand and stuffed them into his pocket where they made a sagging, heavy weight.

The colonel said: "Childress, for that six hundred dollars I've bought your loyalty and your time for four months or until the job is done. Don't forget it. I want evidence against every man who misbrands or butchers any cattle belonging to any member of the Wyoming Cattlemen's Association. I want evidence strong enough to convict. Is that clear?"

"You'll get what you've paid for," Roan said, and whirled toward the door.

Angrily he stomped down the hall and flung open the door of his and Tolan's room, thereby confronting a startled sheriff and a tense deputy.

The sheriff scowled at him and said: "Lyle Weeks was found shot to death out by the Rustler Creek bridge a while ago."

"So?"

"Did you kill him?"

71

Roan hooked his right hand in his belt a couple of inches from the butt of his gun. He made his stare deliberately challenging. "And if I did? Is self-defense a crime in this country? He had his gun in his hand, didn't he? He was shot from the front, wasn't he?"

"You seem to know."

Roan waited. The sheriff was a man of medium size, perhaps sixty years old, whose face in both texture and color suggested weathered saddle leather. His cavalry mustache was snowy white, his eyes a washed-out shade of blue. Roan sensed an uncertainty in the sheriff, an inadequacy that seemed to increase under the pressure of his cold, steady regard. He judged that here was a man too slight for the job he held, at least in these times of impending violence. So he waited, and watched the sheriff begin to break.

The lawman's glance fell away first. Palely angry, studying the polished toes of his boots, he said: "The law requires me to obtain a statement from every suspect even though it's a clear-cut case of self-defense. Did Weeks draw first?"

Behind the sheriff, the deputy snorted: "Damn it, let's haul this hardcase in. The settlers. . . ."

The sheriff shook his head. Suddenly Roan felt pity for man who wore the star. He said: "Sheriff, he wouldn't let it go. He tried to pick it up in the barbershop, as you probably know. And he tried to pick it up again out by the bridge. I just beat him to it, that's all."

He saw relief come over the sheriff's face. The sheriff's tone missed being abjectly grateful. "Well, that settles that, then. I figured it happened about that way. You're in the clear with me, but you'll have to appear for the inquest. All right?"

Roan nodded. He noticed Tolan, grinning sardonically at him from his reclining position on the bed. "I'm taking a job with Manette," he said. "You'll find me out there, if you want me."

The sheriff sighed. "Ah, then you are here to make trouble. Damn it, why does trouble have to bring in so many like you?" He turned to his deputy. "Come on, Sam."

They went out into the hall. Tolan laughed silently as he listened to them wrangling just outside the door, the deputy angry, the sheriff defensive.

"Don't be so hard on the old man," Childress said. "The settlers put him in this job, but the big outfits are piling on a hell of a lot of pressure. And he's getting old. Age takes something out of a man, Earl."

Tolan swung his legs over the side of the bed and sat up. He had sobered and now he looked a little ashamed.

Roan found his Durham sack and shook flaky grains of tobacco into a brown paper. "You eaten yet?"

Tolan shook his head.

"Maybe we can still get something," Roan said. "Let's go see."

Tolan got up and slouched to the door. Roan blew out the lamp and followed, closing the door firmly behind him.

VII

Childress and Tolan were up at dawn. During the night, the snow had stopped, and the clouds had blown away to southward. The fire in the stove had long since gone out, and the room was icy. Shivering, Childress pulled on his trousers and slipped into his boots. His breath made a cloud in the room, a steamy cloud that was slow to dissipate.

The wash water had frozen solid in the bottom of the china pitcher. Tolan wheezed: "Lordy, and I thought Montana was cold."

Childress belted his gun around his middle and shrugged into his plaid woolen shirt. "I'd say it was close to thirty below this morning. I sure wish I had some hot wash water."

He opened the door, almost colliding with an Indian woman who carried a steaming bucket of water. She came into the room and poured both pitcher and wash pan full, stolidly ignoring both Childress and Tolan. Then she padded out again.

Tolan rubbed his stubbled face thoughtfully. He muttered: "I'm not going to shave or cut my hair, so help me, until the grass turns green." He went to the wash pan, lathered his face and neck, and rinsed noisily.

Childress watched him. He had known Tolan for several years, yet in that time he had learned nothing whatever about the man. Tolan simply did not talk about himself. Tolan stood a couple of inches shorter than Roan, and thin, as if his stringy body refused to afford a padding of fat for his flat, hard muscles. His hair and beard were a dark, golden brown, his eyes tiny, close-set, and almost black. His face was sharp and pointed, his teeth slightly protruding. At rare times, when something amused him and his eyes sparkled, Tolan bore a certain resemblance to a chipmunk. Yet withal, there was an economy of movement about him, an instinctive wariness that told Roan plainly that Tolan could be a very dangerous man.

Tolan dried himself on the thin hotel towel and emptied the wash pan into a bucket on the floor. Roan poured it full again from the pitcher. This warmer water took the sleepiness from his eyes and refreshed him. He crammed his hat down onto his head and slipped into his sheepskin. He said: "We'd just as well get out to Manette's this morning."

Tolan nodded. Then he made a sour sort of grin at Roan. "Bothers you, doesn't it . . . this spying, this pretending to be something you're not?"

Roan nodded. "I keep telling myself they're rustling, that they deserve to be caught. I keep telling myself that, if they're not stealing cattle, they've got nothing to fear from us."

"But it still goes against the grain?"

"Yes. Manette's friendly. I like him. If I have to turn him in, I'm afraid I won't soon forget it."

"Well, I respect you for that," Tolan said. "And you'll not be hurting Manette, looks like. You saw yesterday how little chance there is to convict rustlers in this county."

"That bothers me, too. If Houston can't convict them, why is he still so anxious to get evidence against them?"

"He'll make a stab at getting 'em tried in some other county. He's got the Cheyenne courts in his hip pocket, I expect."

Roan sighed. "I'm hungry. Let's go down."

He preceded Tolan down the stairs, trying to take comfort in the reflection that rustlers were directly responsible for his present predicament, and that, ironically, rustlers would extricate him from it whether they liked it or not.

The hotel dining room had begun to fill, and the air was rich with the warming, heartening odors of coffee, flapjacks, and ham. Roan saw Guthrie sitting with Colonel Houston and his daughter at one of the tables. He nodded and smiled at Janet. The colonel stared at him coldly, showing no recognition. But Janet flushed prettily at his sustained and admiring stare.

At another table, Zulke and Russ Conover nodded at Roan with wary caution. They believed him to be on the settlers' side, but couldn't be sure.

Tolan found a vacant table and pulled out a chair. A plain girl of seventeen or eighteen approached with two glasses of water and asked with bored monotony: "What'll it be, gents?"

Roan said: "Flapjacks and ham will do for me. And coffee."

Tolan grunted—"The same."—in a preoccupied tone. Roan followed his glance and felt a stir of surprise. At a table ten feet from them sat a young woman who certainly deserved all of the attention Tolan was giving her. She had jet-black hair, done in a knot behind her head from which straying tendrils escaped. Her skin was smoothly white, her eyes a deep shade of blue. But her lips, too red to be natural, and her dress instantly gave away her calling. "Respectable" women did not wear low-cut bronze satin dresses in the morning.

Her expression held Roan's attention, for it was worried, nervous, expectant. He followed her uneasy glance to the door and saw a man entering. The man paused there a moment, sweeping the room with his arrogant stare. His eyes settled on the girl and began to glow. Although he didn't top medium height, the fellow had the build of a wrestler. The man's head was round and bald as a bullet and his scalp was deeply tanned, as was his heavy-jowled face in spite of the season. His thick, smiling lips somehow seemed too sensual for a man.

Roan looked at the girl again. Pale and taut, she awaited the man's coming with something akin to terror.

"He's got her plumb scared to death," Tolan muttered.

Roan wondered why, and studied the girl's features for his answer. That face didn't suggest beauty at first glance, yet it seemed to become beautiful as you studied it. It was a tired face, one that held too much wisdom, too much knowledge of the world and its ways, but that had been neither hardened nor coarsened by the knowledge.

The man came up to the table and put his stubby, powerful hands on a chair back. Roan saw them knot and tighten. He heard the heavy, angry tones of the man's voice over the babble in the dining room. "Where the hell have you been? What's the idea running out like that?"

Roan felt a stir of disillusion. This sounded like an old, old story, and a sordid one.

But the girl's voice, so clear, so carefully controlled, dispelled his disillusion at once. "Saul Hubner, let me alone. There are people here who. . . ."

Roan came to his feet with a single smooth motion, seconds ahead of Tolan. He took the half dozen steps that separated him from the pair and asked softly: "Your wife, mister?"

The thick-set man looked up at him. "No," he said. "What the hell business is it of yours, anyway?"

"I just wanted to make sure I wasn't interfering between husband and wife," Roan said. "Since you're not married, I'm making it my business. The lady said she wanted to be let alone. Let her alone."

The man called Saul straightened, his hands balling into fists, his shoulders hunched like those of a bear. Not as tall as Roan, he nevertheless appeared enormous by comparison. Roan experienced a sudden uneasiness—not because he feared the man or doubted the outcome, but because he knew it must be a long, dragged-out fight that would empty the dining room and wreck its furniture. And lower him in Janet Houston's eyes, too, he thought miserably. He hated to let her see him brawling in public, apparently over a dance-hall girl. But no withdrawal was possible now. The thing had started. He looked past Hubner at the girl. Her eyes were wide with fright. Deliberately he grinned at her.

Hubner's fist landed high on his forehead with the force of a sledge. Roan staggered back, crashed into a table, and fell, scattering chairs like pins in a bowling alley. He sat up, dazed, and saw Tolan moving in. He said—"No!"—and forced himself up to his feet. Hubner was grinning, his face flushed, and he stepped toward Roan with the obvious intention of finishing this quickly.

But the restraint had gone out of Roan. Freed from his worry over shocking Janet, his concern for the dining-room furniture, he stood there, loose and ready. Hubner came blundering in, swinging wildly. Roan stepped inside and brought a vicious left hook up to the man's throat. Hubner choked, gasped frantically for breath, and failed to get it. Roan stepped close to hit him again and caught one of Hubner's thrashing elbows on the side of his neck. Instantly all light faded from his eyes. His head reeled. His body felt paralyzed. Spread-legged, he stood, waiting for his vision to return, unable to avoid the clutching, grasping hands of his adversary. Hubner's huge arms, almost as thick as an ordinary man's leg, closed about his body and tightened down, crushing his ribs, forcing the air from his lungs with an explosive gasp.

Hubner was still gasping for breath, but he had a saloon brawler's instinct, which was never to stop fighting until you are dead. Back, back he forced Roan's body in a tightening arc that could end but one way, with a broken spine for Roan. Roan felt his ribs crack under the terrific pressure of Hubner's arms.

Panic gave Roan strength. He raised a foot and brought his boot heel down savagely upon Hubner's instep. He felt the pressure go slack, and was able to bring his knee up with brutal force. Hubner's arms dropped free. Roan stepped back. Hubner doubled like a jackknife with the pain in his groin, and Roan brought a smashing uppercut against his jaw. Hubner's doubling movement lent the blow added force, and it snapped his ponderous head up, straightening him.

Roan dimly heard the shouting confusion in the dining room, dimly heard a woman's scream. Then he sent his right fist smoking into the big man's midriff where it sank nearly out of sight.

Hubner's face turned sickly gray. His mouth hung loose and slack. His eyes were dull. Roan was panting from exertion, but he managed a small smile. "Sick?" he asked. "Maybe your breakfast didn't agree with you. You'd better go home and lie down."

Saul straightened with an effort, saying nothing. His eyes fixed Roan with a hate-filled glare, but then he turned and shambled away, grunting softly with pain as he walked.

Roan heard the girl's voice: "You shouldn't have done that."

He grinned at her. "Why not? It needed doing, didn't it?"

"He'll make trouble for you."

"Like he did just now?" He pulled out a chair and straddled it, smiling and panting.

"I'm glad you did it." Her smile lightened the somberness of her face and made her look almost girlish. Roan liked her. She said, as though he had earned an explanation: "Saul owns the Custer Saloon. I've been singing down there, but . . . well, anyway, I quit and took a room here at the hotel. Saul wants me to come back and I don't want to."

Roan was vaguely conscious of movement near him. Glancing up, he saw Houston and his daughter threading their way between the scattered chairs. Janet's face seemed set and cold and she looked away quickly. Roan, perversely annoyed, turned back to the girl across from him and asked: "What's your name?"

"Beth. Beth MacPherson."

"I'm Roan Childress." He nodded at Tolan, whose breakfast had been served and who was eating it with studious concentration. He said: "That's Earl Tolan. I think he'd like to meet you." Beth said nothing, so Roan called: "Earl!"

Tolan raised his head, scowling.

Roan said: "Come here a minute."

Tolan got up, his scowl fading. He came over to Beth's table and Roan said: "Earl Tolan, Beth MacPherson. Earl wanted Hubner, but I beat him to it." He stood up, grinned mockingly at Earl, and said: "I'm hungry. Do you mind if I . . . ?"

Earl said—"No."—his eyes on the girl.

Roan went back to his table and sat down. The waitress brought his breakfast at once and he began to eat, covertly watching the pair at the nearby table. He was almost finished when Earl returned.

Tolan sat down, grinned sheepishly at Roan, and returned his attention to the girl. Tolan's expression surprised Roan. His eyes were filled with loneliness, with yearning, and Roan suddenly glanced away, embarrassed. This was the first glimpse, however slight, that he'd had of the inner working of Tolan's mind. Tolan was not, then, as bitter and taciturn as he seemed. It was in him to look at a dance-hall girl the way most men look at their sweethearts. It was in him to look beyond the shell of disillusion, beyond the marks that life had left.

Tolan said: "Roan, there's times when I'm damned if I ain't ashamed of bein' a man. Who draws the line that separates the good women from the bad? Who the hell sets himself up as God Almighty long enough to do it?"

"I've wondered about that myself," Road said. "The lines are there all right, but damned if I know who draws 'em. I've met women in a dance hall I'd sure prefer to some I've met in church. I guess there's good and bad on both sides of the line."

Tolan muttered, still watching the girl: "Now there's a damned nice girl. Her eyes are soft. She knows how to smile, but I doubt she has much to smile about."

"She's left the Custer. Maybe she's trying to get out of the rut."

"What chance is there of that? Who'd let her? There's that damned Saul Hubner, wanting her to come back. He'll hound her until. . . ." Tolan's jaw worked angrily. "And there's the people on this side of the town. You think they'll let her in?"

Roan said soothingly: "Earl, you never saw her before this morning."

Tolan's grin was rueful. "No," he admitted, "I didn't, did I?" He attacked his cold breakfast with sudden vigor.

Zulke and Conover finished their breakfast and came past the table. Zulke paused and said to Roan: "I understand you're going to work for Manette."

Roan nodded. From the corner of his eye he noticed Conover pausing at the girl's table. He saw her face flush with anger as Conover spoke. She shook her head vigorously. Roan looked quickly at Tolan. Tolan was watching Conover coldly. Roan said: "Ready, Earl?"

Tolan nodded and gathered his feet under him preparatory to rising. Zulke said—"See you."—and headed toward the door, with Conover following closely behind.

Roan got up. The girl at the table gave him a very warm, grateful smile that he returned automatically. He headed toward the door, conscious that Tolan had not missed this exchange, conscious also that Tolan was staring at him with something closely resembling dislike. He thought—*He's jealous.*—and was struck with the ridiculousness of that. But he could not deny its truth. Maybe Tolan had met the girl for the first time today. Maybe it was silly of him to be jealous. But his jealousy was there and it could be an added hazard to their mission here.

Outside, the air was still and bitterly cold. Smoke rose lazily from each chimney in town, forming a sort of motionless pall over it, a fragrant pall for most of the townspeople burned cedar in their stoves. Frosty clouds of steam blew out before Childress and Tolan, and, each time they breathed, the cold clutched at their tender nose membranes as though freezing them with each breath.

They stepped off the walk into the frozen, snowy street, heading for the livery barn. Tolan buttoned his sheepskin tightly around his throat and shoved his hands into his pockets.

It was a little warmer inside the stable, but not much. The horses' bodies made a little heat, amounting in the aggregate to perhaps ten degrees. Roan found his horse and Tolan's and slipped on their bridles.

Frost had condensed on the horses' long, shaggy hair. Roan brushed his own animal's back with his hand where the saddle would go, then flung it up.

He led the prancing horse into the street, grunted—"Let's go."—and swung into the saddle.

The horse bowed his neck, arched his back, and began to buck the cold from his body. When he finished, he broke away and ran like the wind down the wide, uneven street.

An involuntary yell broke from Roan's lips, and then he hit the limits of the town and let his horse run along the narrow road. Behind him, Tolan yanked up his horse's head, thus stopping that bone-breaking crow-hopping, and sank his spurs hard. Tolan had broken horses for a living during one period of his life. He had taken too much of this and now it hurt him intensely to ride a bucking horse. Tolan followed Roan, a hundred yards behind.

A mile down the road Roan drew his horse to a steaming, blowing halt short of the Rustler Creek bridge. After that they rode at a trot, side-by-side.

The sun came out on the gray and white eastern plain. A sizable herd of antelope raced away from their jogging approach. The sky turned a deep, unbelievable shade of blue, and light, fluffy clouds blew across it. But the cold lingered, seemingly unaltered by the sterile rays of the winter sun.

They passed shaggy, thin cattle, and a herd of horses that stared at them incuriously. Crossing a wandering creek, they surprised a buck deer that had lost his left antler and the big animal bounded away in great jumps. A coyote slinked snarlingly from his jack rabbit kill, and in the far distance a bull bellowed a deep, hoarse challenge.

This way they rode, across the empty miles toward the hundred and sixty acre claim of Philo Manette.

VIII

The early morning rush in the hotel dining room had abated somewhat. A waitress came over and began to right the chairs that had been overturned during the fight. The other patrons began to leave, their preoccupation with their own affairs testifying to the fact that disturbances were not uncommon, even in the hotel dining room.

Yet Beth MacPherson lingered at her table, unmoving except for an occasional sip of her cold coffee, and fully aware of the scrutiny she received from each departing group. Gradually Beth's expression settled into something closely resembling despair. *What now?* she asked herself. *You've quit the Custer and you have a room here in the hotel. But you haven't got a job and they wouldn't let you work at it if you did have.* Saul Hubner would hound her until she either went back to the Custer or left Antelope Junction altogether. Oh, he'd go easy for a while, but he'd put the pressure on quickly enough when she came back. She shuddered. She was afraid of Saul. Saul was the kind. . . . Suddenly she wondered: *What kind of man is he, really?* The question made her mind drift back, remembering the first time she had met him. How different he had seemed then.

Beth's father, Ike MacPherson, her mother, and herself, then seventeen, had been a part of the last great migration of settlers. Everywhere they went, it seemed, they found the best land taken, the remainder too dry, or too rocky, or too poor for farming. And as they traveled, searching, failing, something had gone out of her father. He weathered and aged, like their rickety wagon. Each broken wagon tongue, each worn-out steel tire, each lame horse seemed to take a little more out him, until he became an old man, stooped of shoulder, broken of spirit, dull of eye. In each town, each settlement, they had met the same treatment from the inhabitants—ridicule, suspicious contempt, outright dislike. And Beth, growing more beautiful every day in spite of her patched clothing, grew to expect another kind of treatment. Leers from the men, sly remarks, clutching hands. She found that men of the frontier did not want a ragged rawhider's daughter for a wife. She found that she was in a special class, neither good woman nor bad, but something unpleasantly in between.

Her father died somewhere on the high Wyoming plains of snakebite received as he knelt beside the wagon to grease a dry axle. And his death seemed to steal all reason from her mother. With the help of a passing cowboy, they brought Ike Mac-Pherson's body to Antelope Junction and buried it. And there they were, penniless and without means of support.

Saul Hubner came along then. Beth remembered his kindness, his helpfulness. He had seen that they had a house to live in, groceries delivered to the door. He had tried to comfort her after her mother died, less than a month after her father. He had offered her a job, singing in the Custer. Her voice, even then, had possessed a certain bell-clear vibrancy that made men think of other times and other places with sentimental nostalgia. She'd taken the job, of course. What else was there for the ragged daughter of a dead rawhider.

Saul had let her alone for a while, but not for long. He began to try to maneuver her into being alone with him, and, when she avoided him, he became surly and dangerous. Saul demanded certain personal services from all the girls in the Custer.

This was not the first time Beth had quit. She had tried it three times before. But never could she find anything else that would support her, and always upon Saul's assurances that he would let her alone, she had gone back to the Custer. *You were foolish,* Beth decided, *to think you could change this life that you seemed to have slipped into. Life put you into a certain groove very early along the way and made sure you stayed in the same groove until you died.* Yet in spite of her present depression, Beth did not really believe this. Life had been harsh with her, but it had not been able to kill her optimism altogether. She had been unlucky so far, that was all. Somewhere, sometime, she would find a man who would see beneath the exterior of her occupation and background, who would see her as a decent human being. Somewhere there had to be a man who would want her as a wife.

From a corner of her eye, she caught movement near her table. Saul Hubner had returned. He pulled out a chair and sat down.

"Who the hell was that one?" he said.

Beth said: "The big one was Roan Childress. The other was Earl Tolan. They're both strangers in town. At least I haven't seen them before."

Saul made his mouth smile. He said: "Come back to work, Beth. The place ain't the same without you singing in it."

Beth said: "Saul, you never have played fair with me. Not from the very first." She studied him carefully. "I used to think you helped my mother and me out of kindness. But there's no kindness in you, is there, Saul? You did it even then because you wanted me. Only at first you were afraid, because I was only seventeen. So you made me grateful to you for your help and kindness. You gave yourself a hold over me because I couldn't forget it."

"I helped you because I wanted to help you," he said. "Now, Beth. . . ."

"No, Saul. I'm not coming back. I'm tired of your badgering, and I'm afraid of you. Somehow I'm going to get another kind of job. I can sew. I can. . . ."

"And who will let you? Have you tried getting another kind of job, Beth? Do you know what will happen? Every man you meet up with will try to fix it so he's alone with you. And every woman will hate you because she'll know what her man's up to."

"They're not all like that. There are some. . . ."

"Have you ever found any? Be your age, Beth. You're twenty-two. You've knocked around all over the West with that sodbustin' pa of yours and you've been in the Custer damn' near five years. If you've failed to find what you're looking for in twenty-two years, do you think you'll find it now? Come back to work. I'll let you alone."

Beth stared at him. His eyes were hot, belying his words. His lips were slack and loose. And she saw him suddenly as he really was, not a strong man at all, but an inner weakling, a man so unsure of himself that he had to conquer every woman he met. Beth had resisted him for five years, and in this lay the answer to his unceasing lust for her. The old despair stirred in Beth. But she knew he spoke the truth. No other course was open to her—at least not yet. She nodded wearily. "All right, Saul. I'll come tonight."

But she had made her mind up about one thing. She wouldn't just resist this time. She would plan, and save, and, when she was ready, she would leave in the night without a word to anyone. Her debt to Saul, if any, had been paid long ago. She was sick of him, sick of thinking of him. She said: "Go away, Saul, before I change my mind." He started to protest, his voice ugly and thick. Beth said quietly: "I mean it, Saul."

He got up. Beth knew he was giving no ground as he said: "All right. Tonight then." He stared down at her and what she saw in his eyes put a chill into her heart. Then, turning, he lumbered out of the hotel.

Still Beth did not leave, although her coffee cup was empty. For she was thinking of the stranger who had intervened with Saul in her behalf. Not a handsome man, this Childress, but a virile one, in whose face shone both kindness and humor. Her pale skin flushed as she thought of him, of the respectful way he had treated her in spite of her dress, her obvious occupation. But she shrugged, rather helplessly, remembering others like Roan who had treated her with the same sort of kind indifference and she thought bitterly: *What's the matter with me? The ones I want I can't attract, and the ones I attract I don't want.* There had been Conover, who mentioned marriage and fooled her for a while. Conover had no intention of marrying anyone, but wasn't above using the offer of marriage as a bribe. Now there was this Tolan. Beth recalled the almost dog-like way Tolan had watched her. She could not recall ever having seen that particular look in the eyes of a man before.

Smiling faintly, she got up and walked out of the dining room. She climbed the stairs to her room, and the smile faded. She began to pack, for tonight she must go back to her room over the Custer Saloon.

IX

In late morning, Roan Childress and Tolan rode into the yard at Philo Manette's and found the bearded owner repairing a sagging barn door. Roan grinned and offered his hand.

"Tolan and I decided to take you up on your offer of a job," he said.

Manette took his hand. Again Roan was impressed by the man. He liked the classic perfection of Manette's features beneath his trimmed black beard, the steady regard of his eyes, the sure, confident stance he took, legs spread, head and neck thrust slightly forward. "Did you tell him the job would likely end up in a fight?" Manette asked.

Roan nodded. Tolan said cryptically: "Winter jobs are scarce, and we've fought before."

Manette grinned. "Don't you want to know who you're going to be fighting, and why?"

Tolan shrugged and returned the grin. Roan studied his friend, amused and puzzled. Tolan who always stood aloof, waiting for the other fellow to make the initial move of friendship, was meeting Manette halfway.

Tolan said: "Big outfits, I take it. Grab-all outfits."

"That's right." Manette fished a sack of Durham from his pocket and offered it to Tolan. Tolan selected a paper and filled the tiny trough it made in his hand with flake tobacco. He handed the sack to Childress, who also began to build a smoke.

Manette squatted down against the barn, facing the full bright light of the sun, squinting. He said companionably: "Hunker down here and I'll fill you in on what's been happening around here the last few years."

Roan and Tolan dismounted and squatted against the barn. Roan struck a match, held it to the tip of Tolan's cigarette, then to his own. Here in the shelter of the barn wall, he could feel the sun's welcome heat seem to penetrate his sheepskin, his flesh, warming his very bones.

Manette was talking, and Roan yanked his straying thoughts back with an effort. Manette said: "Eastern and British capital is mostly to blame for all the troubles, I reckon. Local outfits sold out to them big muck-a-ducks when times were bad, painting a rosy picture of what they had to sell. When the big boys got here, they were naturally a mite disappointed. They'd bought a lot more than they got. So, being what they were, they set out to rectify that in a way they'd done often enough before. By taking. By grabbing. They brought in a bunch of hardcases like Ransom Coates and they strung line camps and cattle all over Corbin County. Well, things went along that way for a while, the little men muttering but not doing much about it. Then they began to exclude the smaller outfits from their roundups. As a result, we began to lose cattle. A couple of the more reckless ones took it onto themselves to protest, figuring to back up their protests with force if need be. Those were brought home across their saddles, dead. After that, there wasn't any more trouble, open trouble anyway."

Roan said: "Tough game to beat. What did you do?"

"What could we do? Some of the boys commenced to replace

their cattle losses at the expense of the big outfits."

Glancing at Roan, Tolan said succinctly: "Rustling."

"Call it that if you want," said Manette, "and maybe it went beyond strict replacement of losses suffered. Maybe it got to be a way of expressing resentment and helplessness."

"But rustling just the same," Tolan insisted, still for Roan's benefit.

"Yes, rustling," Manette admitted. He added then in a voice that held no particular pride: "I didn't go along with them. I didn't join in what they were doing." He looked straight at Tolan now. "But I'm going to. I'm going to now because it's the only way. I won't ask you boys to go along with me in that. But I want you around to protect this house and my wife when I have to be away." He fell silent, staring at the ground between his booted feet. At last he said: "Well, I've given it to you as straight as I can. Now it's up to you to make your choice."

Tolan asked, deliberately taunting: "How do you know we're not a couple of range detectives on Houston's payroll, just here to get evidence against you?"

Manette smiled. "It wouldn't matter if you were. Because now Houston is helpless. He can't convict a rustler in Corbin County to save his life."

"Then it's going on?" Roan asked thoughtfully. "On a bigger scale than before?"

"It's going on," Manette said, "until they holler uncle. You can bet your life on that." Manette stood up. "You boys can finish hanging this barn door if you want. There's a meeting been called at Zulke's for noon, and I've got to be leaving if I want to get there in time."

Tolan said: "Sure, go ahead. Anything special you want done after we're through with this?"

"You can fix fence." He waved vaguely toward the east. "Try the east line first. It's the worst." He grinned, including them both, and moved away toward the corral. He roped out a big blue roan and saddled him deftly. He led the animal over to the house, left him, and went inside, presumably to tell his wife that Roan and Tolan would be here for dinner. When he came out, he mounted and rode away.

Roan and Tolan blocked up the barn door, and Tolan began to nail the hinges in place with heavy spikes that he clinched on the inside. They worked with quiet concentration and little talk. With that job finished, they picked up fencing tools, mounted their horses, and rode across the snowy field to the east line fence.

As they tightened the barbed wires of the fence, Roan noticed that Tolan wore a dreamy expression. Then Tolan began to talk.

"You know, I keep thinking of that girl in the hotel."

"The saloon girl?"

Tolan's face showed a stir of anger. "Don't call her that."

"Why not? It's what she is."

"Maybe. But she's not like the others. There ain't no hardness in her. I used to know a girl like her, a long time ago. She didn't work in a saloon then, but she does now. They pushed her into it."

Roan kept still, hoping Tolan would go on.

Tolan mused: "You know, it's damned funny the things that happen to people that make 'em what they are. Take me, for instance. Take Ruth Gilroy, the girl I'm talking about. She was friendly, but she wasn't bad. Not a bit. But they got to talking about her down at the pool hall and around the stables. She was older than me, so I never went with her. But I had a crush on her all the same. A bad crush, so's I couldn't believe that she went out at night in the boys' buggies with them."

Tolan drove a fence staple with unnecessary violence.

"I guess I won't ever forget that one morning. I was wandering around town without much to do and stopped to listen to a bunch talking in front of the pool hall. There was one young guy named Frank O'Mara. A ladies' man from the word go. He was talking about having Ruth Gilroy out in his buggy the night before. He was telling all the things he done with her, and how she liked it, too. I was seventeen. And I was stuck on Ruth. I went crazy mad. I jumped O'Mara, and he beat the hell out of me, laughin' like crazy and teasin' me about being stuck on a girl like Ruth."

Now, suddenly, Tolan's leathery complexion whitened with violence of this memory. He tightened a strand of barbed wire with his hammer, and tied it to the post. Roan thought he was through talking, but then Tolan said: "Know what I did? I went home. I got my dad's six-shooter and stuck it in my belt. I went back down to the pool hall and told Frank he was a lying son-of-a-bitch." Tolan laughed harshly. "I was a skinny kid. I was homely and kind of shy. Frank was a lot older. I figured he was a man, but I can see now that he was just another scared kid like I was. Frank wore a gun and he pulled it. Some way or another I beat him." Tolan's face was the color of ashes and his hands shook. "You never quite forget the first one, do you? I still feel sick when I think about how he looked, laying there in the dust, dead. There was a stain of blood spreading out on his white shirt front, and a crowd collecting, looking at me like I was something horrible. I ran. I ran home and got my dad's fastest horse out of the stable. I saddled up and stuffed some food into the saddlebags, cookies mostly." Tolan eked out a spare grin. "Then I rode. I damned near killed the horse. I should never have got away. Hell, I didn't have any experience at that kind of thing, and the sheriff did. But I guess the sheriff didn't care much for the pressure the O'Mara family was putting on him. And he'd always kind of liked me. I reckon I got away because he wanted me to get away."

Roan asked softly: "What happened to Ruth?"

Tolan grunted. "That's the one part I'm sorry for. The town crucified her reputation after that happened. She left town. I ran into her years later in Dodge City workin' as a percentage girl. She didn't even know me. But I guess I was mostly to blame for her turnin' out like she did."

"I doubt that," Roan said. "Seems to me people do what they're meant to do without much help from anyone else."

"Yeah, but without me, she might've married some guy and stayed there in the Klamath Valley."

"And without her, you'd never have started packing a gun."

"No, I guess not."

With that, Tolan reverted to his habitual taciturnity. Yet Roan had learned more about him in this one afternoon than he had in all the years he had known Earl. He knew now how Tolan had come to live by his gun. He had discovered that human understanding and compassion lay beneath his shell of toughness.

The air warmed, the job went on, and behind them Childress and Tolan left a fence that was taut and strong. Noon came, and a woman over at the house, Manette's wife, banged on the bottom of a dishpan with a heavy spoon.

They went in for dinner.

X

The days, filled with toil from dawn to dusk, passed pleasantly. Working for Manette was almost like working for yourself, because he gave no orders and made few suggestions. Roan and Tolan simply saw things that needed doing, and did them. So, as time wore on, Manette's place began to assume a tight and tidy look it had never had before.

Roan thought that Lilac Manette, Philo's wife, who at first had been faintly hostile, was becoming reconciled to his and Tolan's presence. He suspected that now she even welcomed it.

But Roan also knew that something big was shaping up. Conscious of his obligation to Houston, he saddled up late one night and followed Manette when he left to attend a meeting at Zulke's.

Trailing well behind, he came over the low ridge above Zulke's run-down place well after the meeting had begun. He left his horse tied to a cedar and moved down silently, Indian fashion, until he was within earshot of the open-air meeting.

He had little fear of discovery. A fire was blazing in the middle of Zulke's yard and the settlers, perhaps thirty or forty of them, were grouped around it. Roan recognized Russ Conover, the Jiminez brothers, Ramon and Carlos, as well as Ernie Cassel. Manette's horse stood tied to a corral pole and Roan could see him near the fire, a big, bearded man whose stance was confident and sure. Zulke's voice boomed: "Philo, damn it, we picked you to head us up, but what we want to know is what the hell you're going to do?"

Manette waited for the crowd's noise to die. He said: "All right. I'll tell you what we're going to do and I'll tell you what's been done. First of all, I'm going to say this. We're going ahead, but I still don't like it. We're hitting them where it'll hurt, but that doesn't make it right."

A voice yelled: "To hell with what's right! What's being done? What's going to be done?"

The crowd roared, and Manette raised a hand for silence. When he got it, he said: "We're all through taking a steer or two here and there. We're all through taking small bunches and driving them to the railroad construction camps. If we're going to hurt this syndicate, we're going to have to do better than that. You picked me to head you and here's what's being done. Houston is the man we're after, but we'll hit him and Jerome Guthrie north of town at the same time because they're both living in the country and they'll know they've been hit. We'll take five hundred head from Houston and the same amount from Guthrie."

For an instant the crowd seemed stunned, aghast at the boldness and audacity of this. Approval was slow to come, but when it did, it burst out, wholehearted and noisy. The men chattered loudly among themselves, but finally Russ Conover shouted the inevitable question.

"Philo, what the hell are we going to do with a thousand head of cattle? How'll we get rid of them?"

Manette grinned. "We won't, right away. And I'm not going to spill the plan just yet. But don't worry, you can be damned sure Houston will never find them where we're going to take them."

"They'll trail us. Houston will put his gunmen on our trail."

"I doubt it," Manette said. "You boys think I've been sitting on my backside since the trial, doing nothing, don't you? Well, that's not quite the case. Cassel and the Jiminez boys and myself have been busy as hell. We've very carefully and quietly gathered and drifted both bunches of cattle north until they're damn' near to the county line. We've been so careful in fact that the syndicate riders think it's a natural drift. All we've got to do now is wait for a storm to cover our tracks and we'll move them clear out of the county. Houston will think his damned cattle disappeared into thin air."

Murmured approval began within the crowd, but Manette held up his hand again for silence. He said: "When the storm hits, we'll fake raids on every big ranch in the country. We'll move small bunches toward the railroad construction camps. The syndicate's hardcases will be so busy chasing five or ten small bunches that they won't even know the two big bunches are gone until it's too late."

The daring of the plan stirred the imaginations of these men. And Roan knew it would work. By the time the syndicate gunmen realized they had been duped, it would be too late to follow the cattle that had been pointed north, for their trail would be lost in the driving snow. But, watching Manette, Roan thought he detected signs of doubt, of inner conflict, and thought he knew the cause. Manette believed that this all-out rustling offered the only immediate answer to the settlers' problem. Meet force with force. Meet theft with theft. The syndicates had stolen range and grass. Let the little men steal what they were able to steal—cattle. Yet Manette could not fully convince himself that such ruthless measures would produce a permanent solution to the problem. And so Manette was uneasy, fearful that payment would eventually be exacted from every man who participated in the raid.

He started it, though, Roan thought. *He can't stop it now. It's past stopping.*

At 4:00 p.m. on December 20th, Tolan left Manette's and rode toward Antelope Junction. Roan asked him to wait, but Tolan said: "No. I'll see you in town. I've got a date."

Which was not strictly true. He had been meeting Beth regularly, but never by previous arrangement. In early evening it was her habit to get a horse from the livery stable and take a short ride west of town. Since she invariably followed the same route, it was easy for Tolan to intercept her on any evenings he managed to get away early from Manette's.

Tonight, he reined his horse in at the edge of a little thicket of cedars. He did not have long to wait. She saw him and touched her heels to her horse's sides. Her color was better these days, he thought, and she sure did ride pretty. He wished he could be easy and relaxed with her, but he could not. He gave his greeting in a voice tinged with formality, and reined his horse around so that he swung in beside her.

"Nice day for a ride," he said.

"You say that every time you meet me here," Beth told him, but her eyes were gentle and held no mockery.

Tolan muttered embarrassedly: "Seems I can't think of much else to say." He hesitated, and then went on. "I've got lots of things I want to say, but they don't come out." He looked at the sky. "It ain't a nice day. It's going to snow. Maybe it just seemed nice when I saw you."

Beth flushed lightly. "You're improving," she murmured. Her heart was beating rapidly. She thought about what he had just said, and then she added: "In fact, that's one of the nicest things anyone ever said to me."

Her guard, raised against all men, was coming down slowly. At first she had been cold and wary with Tolan. But gradually she found herself thawing, touched by the desperate loneliness so very apparent in him, appreciating the fact that he made no advances and never tried to touch her. But she still didn't like the way he looked at her.

He was doing it now. She said: "Don't look at me like that."

"Like what?"

"Like. . . ." Failing to find the right words, Beth sighed and said: "I don't know. I don't know. But it's different from the way the others look at me. What kind of man are you, anyway? What do you want from me?"

Her questions sounded more blunt than she intended. They turned Tolan's face beet red. He tried several times to speak, swallowed each time, and finally said: "Hell, I ain't no special kind of man. I'm just a man, I reckon. And what does any man want from a woman?"

Beth's eyes turned bitter. She said: "From some women they want many different things, I suppose. But from a saloon girl they want only one thing."

Tolan suddenly bristled. "They been botherin' you? You just tell me who."

Beth eyed the gun he wore. His anger awed her, for it was quiet and terrible. "What would you do to them?" she asked timidly.

He gave her no answer and she needed none.

"You actually would, wouldn't you?" she whispered. "But I wouldn't be worth that." She shook her head, puzzled and confused. This man was a riddle to her, an enigma, something entirely new in her experience. She murmured: "You're making of me something I'm not, something I can never be. You think you see something in me that isn't even there."

"It's there, all right. I ain't making any mistake." He was fiercely argumentative now. "It's the others that's been making the mistake. Only they'd better not make it while I'm around."

His words were those of a boy, yet there was nothing boyish in his tone. Beth said softly: "You know, I think I'm a little afraid of you."

Instantly she wished she hadn't said that. A grimace of pain crossed his face and disappeared. His eyes grew dull and his voice was so low she had to strain to hear. "Don't say that. Don't ever be afraid of me. Because you're the one thing I could never hurt."

Words of apology rushed to her lips, but she never uttered them. They had entered the outskirts of the town, and suddenly Roan Childress stood in their path, grinning.

"Hey! You two quarreling already?"

Tolan scowled at him. But Beth smiled, thankful that an awkward moment had been averted and feeling the pull of Childress's personality in spite of herself. She said: "No. Just talking. I haven't seen you since that day in the hotel dining room and I never really thanked you properly for that."

"Forget it." Roan pulled his horse over beside her and the three of them rode abreast down the street. Beth found herself chattering away to Roan like an excited schoolgirl and was briefly surprised at herself and at him, who could make her feel so at ease. They came to the Custer and Beth dismounted, taking Roan's hand because it was there for her to take.

Then she noticed Tolan's expression, and suddenly the tiniest of chills ran along her spine. For his face had gone gray, and he was looking at Roan with something very close to hatred.

Beth went to him and put a hand on his arm. She said breathlessly: "Thank you for riding with me. Will you come again soon?"

The tension seemed to drain out of him. "Sure, Beth. Sure I'll come. First time I get the chance." And with that husky-voiced reply, the things she had seen in him a moment ago were gone.

She turned and stepped inside the Custer, knowing that it would be all too easy for her to set those two men against each other. And knowing, too, that, if Roan and Tolan ever did become enemies, it would be too great a burden for her conscience to bear.

Standing in the window of the hotel room, Janet Houston saw Roan offer his hand to Beth and help her from her horse. Even at this distance she could make out Beth's pleased and happy smile, and for some reason Beth's smile hurt Janet and made her strangely lonely.

Perhaps her expression was too readable, for Ransom Coates came to the window and peered down into the street. He divined Janet's feelings as soon as he saw Roan. He put a hand on her arm, and turned her toward him.

"I'm not a man you can tease," he said. "Stop trying it."

Janet stiffened. "You give yourself too much credit, Ransom."

"Do I?" He studied her for a moment, realized that he was on the wrong track, and changed it. "Janet, stop putting me off. Set a date and marry me. You don't give a damn about Childress. You've only seen him a couple of times. And you haven't anyone else you're interested in."

That was true, Janet admitted. She also knew why—Coates did not allow her to spend time with anyone else. He frightened off all the men who might become interested in her, chilling them with his deadly reputation. The whole country knew that Coates wanted her and no one else dared to court her. The situation annoyed her, and always had. Yet she had no solution for changing it, and, considering the virile attraction that Coates exerted whenever he wished to, she couldn't even be sure she would force a change if the opportunity arose. Still, this chance to puncture Coates's proprietary arrogance tempted her. She said: "I could become interested in Mister Childress, I think."

She saw his eyes flare. "That drifter?" Coates said harshly. "Why? He's only a damned spy, taking pay from both sides."

Janet controlled her answering resentment, smothered it with taunting sweetness. "You're being vindictive, Ransom. You're annoyed because he was able to take your gun so easily that first day on the courthouse steps."

Coates swallowed audibly. But when he spoke he sounded quite calm. "I'll take care of that before long," he said. "I'll make him wish he'd never seen me."

Abruptly worried, Janet moved away from the window. Putting weariness and resignation into her voice, she said: "Ransom, don't quarrel with me. Please. As you say, I've only seen Mister Childress a couple of times."

He seemed to be placated, and gave her one of his very rare smiles. With a gentleness that was obviously false he said: "This isn't one of our better days. I should go."

Janet returned his smile but she felt relieved when the door closed behind him. She reflected that there was no understanding or peace in their relationship, but always this tension, this sparring. Suddenly tired, she began to get ready to go to dinner.

Indeed, she was foolish to imagine that there could be

anything between herself and Roan Childress. He was, as Coates had said, only a drifter, and apparently a very quarrelsome one at that. But. . . . She had admired him for his defense of her on the courthouse steps. She could not bring herself to approve his defense of Beth MacPherson in the hotel dinning room—if defense it had been—yet she knew she would like to know Roan better. Yes. If a chance to talk to him presented itself, she would take it!

She hummed as she brushed her hair.

XI

Roan watched the door close behind Beth, very much aware of Tolan's jealousy. He was sorry about it, but he did not know how he could have averted it. He had done nothing at all to bring it on.

Tolan reached down and grasped the reins of Beth's horse. He said shortly to Roan—"Coming?"—and, without waiting for an answer, turned away toward the livery stable.

Roan followed, silent, and gradually Tolan's coldness seemed to thaw. He said: "Manette's up to something."

"I know. They're planning a raid that will make everything that's gone before look like nothing."

"What are we going to do about it?"

Roan shrugged. "Houston wanted evidence, didn't he? Well, we'll get it for him. But I draw the line at spilling Manette's plans. I'll get Houston the evidence after the steal is pulled off. I won't help him break it up."

"That's playing it thin, ain't it?"

Roan whirled and snarled: "I like Manette. I hired out to get evidence that can be used in a court of law. The deal didn't include setting him up so Houston's gunnies can kill him."

Tolan's eyes widened slightly. "Don't get on the prod. I'll go along with that."

Roan's mouth twisted wryly. He said: "I've wished a thousand times I'd never seen the colonel. I've wished a thousand times I hadn't taken his money. But I did, and I guess there's no help for it now."

"You know more than you're telling," Tolan said. "What is it?"

"The other night I heard Manette slip out of the house and get a horse out of the corral. I followed him."

"Where'd he go?"

"Zulke's. There was a bunch there." Roan studied Tolan for a moment. Finally he said: "If I tell you what happened, you'll keep it to yourself?"

Tolan's eyes sparkled briefly with resentment. But his tone was quiet enough. "You know me well enough that you hadn't ought to have to ask that."

"I'm sorry. This damned business has got me on edge, I guess." He rode in silence for a few minutes. "But like I said, they're planning a big steal. Five hundred from Houston, five hundred from Jerome Guthrie. He's the red-faced man who was with Houston in the hotel dinning room the day I had that beef with Hubner. They'll mask the big raid by making half a dozen smaller raids. All they're waiting for is a storm."

Tolan squinted at the leaden sky. "They might not have to wait long."

"No. Not very long. Tonight or tomorrow we're going to get it."

"What're you going to do?"

"Follow the big bunch . . . one of 'em anyway. Find out where they go. After that, I'm done."

"What about me? What do you want me to do?"

"Stay at Manette's. He hired us to protect his place while he was gone. There ought to be at least one of us there."

Tolan shrugged. "Whatever you say."

They reached the livery barn and Tolan dismounted. He went inside, leading Beth's horse. Roan waited in the street, scowling and taciturn. In his own thoughts, he had gone this far. He would follow the stolen cattle until he found out where they were taken. He would return to Antelope Junction. After that, he faced a choice. Return Houston's money, or give him the evidence he needed to convict the rustlers and recover the cattle. He didn't know which he would do in the end. He just didn't know, and indecision was torturing him.

Tolan came out and mounted, and they rode back toward the Custer. As they came abreast of the saloon, Tolan reined in to the rail and stepped down. "Drink?" he asked, and Roan laughed. He swung down off his horse and looped the reins around the rail.

The Custer was crowded, mostly with small cowmen, and Roan sensed a tension in the air, probably caused by the cold outside, by the overcast skies, by the imminence of a storm. Off behind the bar, the dance floor looked jammed. Lively music came from a piano player and fiddler at the extreme rear of the saloon.

"She sings her first song at nine," Tolan said. "Wait till you hear her, Roan. Just wait."

Roan checked the clock over the bar. "That's two hours off and I'm hungry. Let's go over to the hotel and eat."

"You go on. I'll get something later. You'll be back before nine?"

"Sure." Roan gave Tolan a friendly cuff on the shoulder and went outside.

The wind was rising ominously and turning cold. The skies were overcast with scudding low clouds and the wind swirled, damp and raw. Roan walked up the street to the Teton Hotel, entered the lobby, and hesitated, thinking of Tolan and of Beth. Suddenly lonely, he wished he did not have to eat alone.

102

Then he felt a light touch on his arm. He swung around, startled, and found Janet Houston standing beside him, looking a little abashed at her own boldness. She murmured: "Good evening, Mister Childress."

"Miss Houston. How are you?"

"I'm very well, thank you. And you?"

"Fine."

The amenities were over and yet she lingered, a flush rising slowly from her proud throat. Roan caught her arm. "Don't go," he said quickly. "Have you eaten yet?"

"No."

"I was just going in. Will you join me?"

A smile hovered on her full, red lips. She said: "I was hoping you'd suggest that. I should wait for Father and he'll probably be angry if I don't. But he won't be down for another half hour and I'm starved."

Roan watched her precede him into the dining room, liking her uncomplicated honesty and wondering why most women should shrink so from a forthright admission that they were hungry. He guessed appetites were not considered lady-like.

He seated himself across from Janet, and the waitress came. Janet smiled at her. "I'll try the roast beef, I think."

Roan said: "The same." The girl went away, and he returned his attention to Janet. She seemed to be studying him with deep interest. Then into her eyes came a serious, worried expression, and something else, something very close to terror.

"What's the matter?" he asked.

She fingered her water glass, hesitating, but then her lips went loose and the guard dropped from her eyes. "I've just got to trust somebody," she said. "It might as well be you."

"I don't understand."

"I think you do. You know what's building up among my father, his friends, and the settlers."

He said cautiously: "What's building up, Miss Houston?"

"Trouble. Terrible trouble. I want you to tell me what's going to happen."

"I can't tell you what will happen. Your father hired Tolan and me to gather evidence of rustling. We're doing it, or trying to."

"And when you get it?"

"We'll turn it over to your father. He'll bring action in the courts against the men we name."

Janet shook her head slowly. "I don't think it's that simple. The trial of Otto Zulke proved that. What good would it do Father to bring them into court if he knew the court would only acquit them?"

"Maybe he'll figure a way to get them tried in another county."

Janet was very pale now. It seemed an effort for her to tear the words from her mind. "I don't think he has any intension of bringing them into court," she said huskily.

"Then he's wasting his money gathering the evidence."

"Is he?" Suddenly her eyes were hooded, blank.

Roan said: "I don't think I understand you."

She made a conscious effort to smile. "Sometimes I doubt if I understand myself." She struggled with her confused emotions quite visibly for an interval. Then more composed, she said: "Mister Childress, I'm a foolish woman. Please forget the things I've said. I am probably mistaken." Beneath her breath, barely audible to Roan, she made the words: "I pray to God I am."

He felt drawn irresistibly to this small, strong girl. He liked her honesty and her lack of feminine coyness. He would have pursued the subject further, but he had no chance. For Ransom Coates came into the dining room and paused, scanning the tables with his pale, dangerous eyes. Roan felt a distinct shock as the man's eyes touched his, for the jealous hate they held was as tangible as the sudden, unexpected blow of a fist. Then Coates came threading between the tables toward him.

Moving by instinctive compulsion, Roan's right hand dropped from the table's edge and hung straight at his side. He thought: *This is no place for trouble. There are too many people.* But he felt better with his sleeve brushing the holstered gun.

Janet asked—"What's the matter?"—and then she saw Coates, too. Roan risked a quick glance at her. She was furious. But she also was afraid. *Why?* he wondered.

Coates came up to the table and spoke in a lowered tone to Roan. "Get up and get out of here." His voice was like the lash of a whip.

For an instant, Roan stared with utter disbelief. Then his anger rose to a white-hot pitch. He came very close to grabbing for his gun, the very move Coates hoped he would make. But reason returned in time, and with it humor. Roan's mouth split into a wide grin. He asked with open mockery: "What do you do when a man won't jump when you tell him to? Or is that something beyond your experience?"

He felt Janet's hand clutching his arm, but he kept grinning, enjoying Coates's white-faced fury, enjoying his abrupt lack of words. He had no idea at all of how it would end, but he found himself unable to stop baiting this arrogant, gun-crazy bastard. The tension had to break. It spread throughout the room. Quickly, furtively people began to rise from their seats and head for the door, scurrying a little in their haste as they moved across the line of fire behind Coates.

It was the waitress who broke the tension. With her attention divided between the tray she carried and the moving occupants of the room, she missed the reason for their hurry. And she failed to recognize Ransom Coates, for his back was to her. Excusing herself in a quick, shy voice, she stepped between

Coates and Roan Childress, bearing her heavily laden tray.

Coates's hand flicked out like the striking head of a snake. It struck the waitress' shoulder and flung her violently aside. She stumbled against a chair and fell, and the tray *clattered* to the floor with an ear-splitting *crash*. The waitress made a low, terrified cry as she sprawled to the floor. Roan palmed his gun and surged to his feet.

He saw Coates hand flash toward his own weapon, and then he flipped the table over, blocking that move. His gun hand rose and whipped down, raking a bloody furrow across Coates's forehead from hairline to nose. Janet Houston backed way, a hand held to her open mouth, her eyes wide with horror.

The slashing blow had staggered Coates, slowing his second attempt to draw. But his gun was coming up, a third time, and its hammer was back. Checking the return upsweep of his Colt's blood-tinted barrel, Roan chopped down again, this time against Coates's gun wrist. Coates howled involuntarily, and his gun fell from his numbed fingers.

Roan laughed. "Now I'm really going to give you something to remember me by," he crooned at the man.

Coates stooped to retrieve his gun. Roan brought his knee up. It smashed Coates's nose, made a pulp of his mouth. And before Coates could recover, Roan's gun slashed along the side of his head. One of Coates's ears began to bleed.

Janet screamed and only this saved Coates from further punishment. Roan shot her a hasty glance, and then brought the gun mercifully down on the top of the killer's skull. Coates slumped to the floor.

The hotel clerk came into the dining room, yelling in a cracked voice: "Go back to your tables, folks! Go back to your tables, please! I've sent for the sheriff and he'll be here in just a minute."

Roan helped the waitress to her feet. He held her up with an arm about her shoulders until Janet took over, murmuring sympathetically: "Are you hurt? Come on upstairs and lie down until you feel better."

After that, Roan righted the two overturned tables, and with exaggerated care placed chairs around them. Janet and the waitress moved away through the crowd toward the lobby.

The sheriff, Gustav Orr, came pushing through, growling irritably, but when he saw Coates on the floor, he went sickly pale. He said: "Mister, get out of town. I'll put Coates in jail overnight, but if you're here after sunup, no power on earth can save you."

"Yeah, sure," Roan Childress said, and walked out into the night.

XII

Tolan had left the Custer before Roan returned and Roan guessed he had gone down the street to a restaurant for his supper. He moved to the bar and downed a drink.

The fight with Coates had stirred up a sour moodiness. Or maybe it wasn't the fight at all, but the things behind the fight. Coates had been jealous, and there must be some basis for his jealousy. Yes, that was it—the bond between Janet Houston and Coates made him feel depressed. He had told himself once that he had no chance with Janet but now he knew her better. There was girl who didn't put much store in material things. She would follow her heart. But where would her heart lead her?

The confused noise of the saloon didn't reach him. He finished his second drink and stared somberly at the empty glass. Occasionally a man spoke to him or slapped his shoulder in passing, but Roan just nodded absently in reply.

The scream made little impression at first. It was another sound in a confused jumble of sound. But gradually the tone of it snagged on his nerves. Roan raised his head and looked around.

A scream, a woman's scream. It sounded like the frantic wail of a lost soul. Rather faint it had been, and its echoes already had died in the air. Roan looked at the bartender, Everett, and said: "Where'd that come from?"

Everett shrugged. The gesture expressed routine boredom, but Roan thought he detected an odd glint in the man's eyes as Everett turned away.

Roan pushed through the crowd, heading for the wide stairway between the bar and the dance floor. He hesitated at the first step. *This is something else that's none of your business,* he told himself. *Stay out of it.* And then he went on, taking the steps two at a time.

At the head of the stairs he heard it again, but this time the scream choked off, as though a hand had been clapped over the screaming woman's mouth. He ran down the dim hallway toward a door at its end.

He flung open the door, stepped into the room, and saw Saul Hubner struggling with a woman in a green silk gown. Hubner's bulk hid most of her body, but as Saul flung his head around to stare at him, Roan caught a glimpse of her face.

He said: "Let her go."

Hubner flung Beth away from him. Beth began to sob brokenly, uncontrollably.

"Hubner, a man that'll force a woman is the dirtiest thing on the face of the earth."

Hubner's face was red with exertion, shining with sweat. "Get out of here," he panted. "Get out before I kill you."

Roan just waited. Hubner glared at him, then eased his hand toward his side coat pocket.

Roan settled slightly, arms loose and relaxed. "Go ahead," he said. "Grab it. I'll put three holes in your belly before you can get it cocked."

Hubner froze. Silence became a dead weight in the stuffy room, and even Beth was still, her eyes wide and horror-stricken. Silence went on and on until its tension became intolerable.

The silence broke Saul Hubner. He dropped his hand to his side and licked his lips like a trapped, desperate animal.

"Get out of here, Hubner."

Hubner swung his ponderous head and looked at Beth. It seemed to shatter Beth's control. She shuddered violently, and then, as if she could do nothing else, she stumbled across the room and threw herself into Roan's arms.

Roan swung her aside and held her with one arm, keeping the other free. He repeated in a slightly louder voice: "Hubner, get the hell out of here!"

Still Hubner did not move. Roan heard running footsteps in the hallway behind him. He knew Hubner was hoping for reinforcements from his saloon crew but he couldn't move with Beth clinging to him so fiercely. He started to turn so he could cover Hubner and the door at once, and then relaxed as Tolan burst into the room, shouting as he came: "Beth, you all right? I heard. . . ." Tolan saw Beth in Roan's arm. He said: "What the hell's going on?"

Roan ignored him. "Hubner," he said, "if you don't get out now, you never will."

Hubner went out like a bull rushing through a half-open gate, jostling Tolan aside as he went.

Tolan asked furiously: "Beth, what the hell you doin' with Roan?"

Beth pushed herself away from Roan, her weeping stilled. She stared at Tolan for an instant, then ran from the room. Tolan did not even try to stop her. His narrowed eyes appraised Roan coldly. "Do you have to have every damned woman you see?"

"Quit jumping to conclusions," Roan said disgustedly. "Hubner was trying to force himself on her. She screamed. I came in and interrupted."

"What was she doin' in your arms?"

"She was scared half to death." Roan watched the sick jealousy slowly drain from Tolan, and, when he judged it had cooled enough, he said wearily: "Better forget her, Earl, if you're as damned suspicious of her as all that. Find yourself an ugly woman that no man will look twice at. Then you can be sure."

He turned his back on Tolan and went out into the hall. There was no sound from Tolan for a moment. Then he heard Tolan's hurrying steps behind him. Tolan said: "Where do you suppose Beth went?"

Roan grunted, still walking.

Tolan said—"Roan!"—and Roan stopped. Tolan muttered: "I'm worried about her." He did not apologize for his suspicions, but Roan knew he was sorry.

Roan said: "Don't worry about her. She'll be all right."

They went on down the stairs and pushed through the crowd to the outside door. Pausing on the walk, they looked up at the sky.

The night was black, and the rawest of winds blew stiffly out of the north. Almost as though their coming from the saloon doorway were a signal, a flurry of snow struck Antelope Junction's main street, obscuring the lamplit windows along its wide length.

A man passed them and went into the Custer, releasing its hubbub into the night air. Roan heard him shout something indistinguishable and almost immediately afterward the door opened again and men spilled from it. They milled around their horses at the rail, then mounted, and rode quickly out of town. Roan recognized the squat shape of Zulke among them and said to Tolan: "It's time. This is the storm they've been waiting for."

He knew he had to leave town at once, yet the idea of leaving now galled him.

"Get the horses," he said. "I want to see Houston."

"Changed your mind about tipping him?"

"No. Not that. I just don't want Coates to think he's run me out."

He shouldered his way through the hotel door and started across the lobby toward the stairs. He pulled up short as he saw Houston's short, belligerent figure blocking his way. He said: "I was looking for you."

"And I was looking for you. You're a damn' troublemaker, Childress. Get out of town. Stay away from Coates or he'll kill you."

"Houston," Roan said, "you're the third tonight that's ordered me to get out of somewhere or other. Now I'll tell you something. Keep your damned killer off my neck. What he got tonight is only a small sample of what he'll get next time he tangles with me. Pass it on to him, Houston."

With that off his chest, he whirled and walked across the lobby to the door.

The storm had lost no time in building up to its full fury. The wind snatched at his breath as he stepped out, whipped his coat open, and tugged at his hat. He caught the flaps of his coat and buttoned it across his chest. He yanked his hat down over his narrowed, angry eyes. He looked upstreet and down, searching for Tolan, who should be back by now with the horses. Then, cursing softly, he headed for the livery barn.

Tolan hesitated after Roan left him. He watched Roan stride up the street and disappear into the Teton Hotel. Roan had said to get the horses. But something else needed doing first. Abruptly

Tolan wheeled and went back into the Custer.

The crowd had been thinned considerably by the departure of the settlers. Tolan hurried to the bar and spoke to Everett Dowd, the bartender: "Where'd Hubner go?"

"He went out, that's all I know. Right after Beth left. What the hell was that all about, anyway?"

"Never mind." Tolan went outside again. He paused on the walk, hardly conscious of the howling wind. *Where would Beth go? Hubner would follow Beth, for sure. But where?*

He discarded the hotel as a refuge for Beth. The hotel would be too obvious. She had mentioned a house, though. She and her mother had lived there when they first came to Antelope Junction. She had pointed it out to him, a vacant house, run-down and unpainted.

Tolan crossed the street at a run, turned the corner, and headed toward the edge of town.

Roan had said Beth would be all right, but Tolan did not believe it. Hubner was not the sort to give up. He'd keep after her until. . . . Running, he muttered aloud: "Until he's dead."

The snow was blinding now. He almost passed the house before he saw it. He charged through the gate, missing neither the small woman prints on the porch, nor the larger prints of a man overlying them. The door hung open, *banging* in the wind. With his boots *squeaking* slightly in the snow underfoot, Tolan eased through it, and into the frigid, barn-like interior.

He was briefly silhouetted against the doorway, and a gun flared across the room, bright and momentarily blinding. Tolan leaped aside. The bullet tore through the door panel, less than an inch from his head.

Tolan grinned humorlessly, sure of his quarry now, and with the hunter's excitement rising in him. He said: "Now it's self-defense, isn't it Hubner? Because you fired first."

That brought another gun flare, another bullet that missed,

this time by at least a yard.

"Where would be a good place to shoot a man that wouldn't leave a woman alone, Hubner? In the belly?" Suddenly he heard an irrational sobbing from the depths of the house. He called: "Beth? It's all right now! He won't bother you again."

He received no answer. But the sobbing seemed to fade, as though by distance, and Tolan heard a board *squeak* somewhere in the rear of the house.

He repeated savagely—"In the belly, Saul?"—and got his answer in the form of two wildly triggered shots. He laughed. He heard the back door slam, and knew Beth had gone out. He said: "Four. Do you carry an empty cartridge under the hammer, Saul? If you do, there's only one. Which is it, Saul, one or two?" Over across the room, Saul was breathing harshly, heavily. Tolan said: "Maybe you know how a woman feels with you after her, Hubner. Come on, shoot. Let's get this over with."

He had his gun in his hand now, the grips cold and hard against his palm. He thumbed back the hammer, which made a loud *click* in the almost complete silence. He said—"I'm coming, Saul."—and took a step out toward the center of the room. Something grated under his foot, and he quickly stepped aside, this time onto a *squeaking* board. These two sounds, so close together, must have been too much for Hubner's crumbling nerves, for he fired.

Tolan did not know where that bullet went. He had no thought for it. As Hubner's gun flashed, Tolan's flipped into line with the flash, then moved right half a dozen inches. His finger tightened on the trigger before the odd afterglow of the flash had disappeared from his eyes. And his own gun roared, unnaturally loud in the closed room. He heard a gasp, a soft grunt, and the *clatter* Hubner's gun made falling to the floor. Then there was a sighing sound as Hubner's huge body slipped down the wall to collapse on the bare floor.

Without a second glance in that direction, Tolan went out the front door, leaving it open and banging behind him. Quickly he circled the house. He picked up Beth's tracks coming out the back door. He followed them until they came to the street, but he lost them immediately then, for drifting snow had covered them over. But it satisfied Tolan, knowing Beth was safe. Holstering his gun, he went back to the livery barn.

He met Roan coming out the door, leading the saddled horses. "Where the hell have you been?" Roan asked irritably. "I thought you went after the horses."

Tolan took the reins of his own animal from Roan's hands. He said: "Hubner chased her half across town to an old empty house where she used to live. I killed him."

Swinging into his saddle, he led Roan out of town at a hard run.

Manette's wife came to the door as they rode into the yard, her face concerned and worried. Roan called—"It's only us, Missus Manette!"—and rode toward the corral as though to put up his horse.

Tolan dismounted at the corral gate, but Roan sat his horse.

"If she asks," he said, "tell her I had supper in town and a few too many drinks. Tell her I've gone to bed."

"All right. Good luck."

"Thanks. If I'm late getting to Zulke's and they've already left, I'll need all the luck I can get."

He rode away at a walk so Mrs. Manette would not hear the pound of his horse's hoofs. But once out of earshot, he sank spurs and lifted the animal to a reckless gallop.

Five miles to Zulke's. He had left town shortly after Zulke had, and so should reach Zulke's place but ten or fifteen minutes behind the man. And, he judged, the settlers would waste at least half an hour talking and making last-minute plans.

Five or six simultaneous raids had to be made on the big ranches, scattered from one end of Corbin County to the other. Besides that, two groups of men must pick up the two large herds that had been partially gathered and drifted northward almost to the county line. In such a complicated operation, last minute planning was inevitable. The small raids didn't interest Childress. They were decoys, nothing else. They would be arranged so that they would be easily detected, so that the gun crews of the big ranches would follow and try to halt them. But when the gun crews reached the stolen herds, they would find only cattle and perhaps a few horse tracks fast drifting over with snow, making pursuit all but impossible. The decoys would immobilize the gun crews, would keep them ignorant of the larger herds being stolen to the north.

Childress smiled grimly at the simplicity and effectiveness of the plan. It would work. And tonight, with luck, he would earn every penny Houston had paid him and be free again, free of this dirty job. For some reason, Janet Houston's fearful words—*I don't think he has any intention of bringing them to court.*—crossed his mind. What on earth made her think that? Why, if he had no such intention, would Houston pay two men $150 each per month to gather evidence of rustling? Why? He shook his head. Janet must be mistaken. She was young and afraid, imagining things.

The insistent cold crept through Roan's heavy clothes, chilling him to the bone. His feet and hands were numb. He dismounted and walked until blood began to pound again in his legs and feet.

Somewhat after midnight, he saw ahead of him the dim, flickering light in Zulke's window. Cautious now, he stepped down and tied his horse securely to a sagebrush root in a spot sheltered slightly from the cold sweep of wind. He stooped and removed his spurs, stuffing one in each pocket of his sheepskin coat so they couldn't jingle. Then he advanced through the icy cross wind, coming up on the cabin at right angles to the gale.

Snow stung the side of his face and turned his ear numb. But as he drew nearer, he could see the milling mass of men and horses in the yard. The door of the cabin kept opening and shutting, and each time it opened the crowd grew larger.

He heard Manette's tight voice. "All right. Ride out. You all know where you're to go. Make your raids between two and five in the morning. And make enough noise about it so's they'll get on your trails, or else the decoy raids won't work."

Roan watched them mount up and ride away in groups. He kept track of Manette and Zulke, though, because it figured that they would lead the two big raiding parties.

Nor was he mistaken. Manette and Zulke waited with half a dozen men each until the last of the others had gone. Then with a low—"Luck."—they mounted up and rode to the north.

Roan made his way back to his horse. He put his spurs on again, mounted, and angled northward to cut the trail of Zulke's party. He threw a last look at the cabin. He saw the lamp wink out, and then all was dark. He cut the snowy trail of half a dozen men and turned into it, facing the full force of the wind now.

He spurred his horse until he heard the *jingle* of spur against cinch buckle, the *squeak* of saddle leather, and the low run of voices. He checked his pace and settled himself in the saddle for a long, cold ride.

XIII

Jerome Guthrie was a big, hearty man in his early sixties. Round and florid of face, he affected burnsides that reached nearly to his chin. Otherwise, except for a small mustache, he was clean-shaven. Three years ago, Guthrie bought the big, sprawling Spur Ranch, twelve miles northwest of Antelope Junction.

Spur's range began just a little south of the huge ranch house, and extended northward to the county line. Although honest enough in his own way, Jerome Guthrie was afflicted with the blindness common to the other large cattlemen who belonged to the Association. He could see only one side of the present controversy—his own side. To his credit, however, he did not subscribe to Colonel Houston's violent views as to its solution. He took no great part in the Association's activities, preferring to send his own hardcase crew against the rustlers. A lone wolf, but no less acquisitive than the other large ranchers, Guthrie had added steadily to Spur range in the last three years. He had taken range to which he had no legitimate claim simply because he felt strong enough to take and hold it. He had a wife, a quiet, sweet-faced woman, and two healthy, rowdy sons, aged nine and five. He also had a son by a previous marriage who was a practicing lawyer in Cheyenne.

Tonight, he left the Whaite Merchantile Store at the lower end of Main, his arms loaded with packages. Behind him came Rufus Whaite, similarly loaded. Guthrie stowed his packages in the rear of his buggy, and helped Whaite do likewise. Whaite, pleased at the size of his sales to Guthrie, called cheerfully as the buggy drove away: "If I don't see you before, Mister Guthrie, Merry Christmas! And the same to your wife and boys!"

"Thanks. Same to you." Guthrie drove up Main, past the Custer, almost past the hotel. Then he got to thinking about the long, cold ride ahead, and murmured to himself: "One for the road."

Smiling, he pulled in toward the hotel and stopped his horse. He climbed down out of the buggy and hooked the cast-iron weight to the horse's bridle to hold him still. He went through the lobby into the bar, and there he had more than one, because he met the colonel and got to talking. They talked about the settlers, and about the weather. They discussed the fight in the dining room and predicted a sure, sudden death for Childress at Coates's hands, when he got out of jail.

So it was after midnight when Guthrie remembered that he still had to drive all the way home. He made his excuses and went out again into the night. His buggy horse was cold from standing, and Guthrie let him out a little as he drove through town. Liquor had put a mellow glow in him, and he found himself anticipating his two sons' joy when they opened the packages he had bought on Christmas morning.

At the very edge of town, his horse came to a sudden, sliding halt and reared high in the air. The buggy tipped dangerously. Guthrie snapped out of his musing trance, shouted a vicious curse, and reached for the whip in the socket beside him. Then he saw the reason for the commotion. A woman stood in mid-street, fighting a fractious horse, her skirts whipping violently in the strong wind. It was these whipping skirts that had frightened Guthrie's horse.

Guthrie climbed down out of his buggy, speaking soothing words to his own and the woman's horse. Coming close to her, he asked, almost shouting in order to be heard: "Ma'am, what the devil are you doing out in this storm?"

"I'm going to Cheyenne." She sounded irrational, nearly hysterical. "If I can get this darned horse quieted down."

Guthrie grinned, recognizing the girl singer at the Custer. He said: "The horse's got more sense than you have, ma'am. He knows you'd never make it alive."

"I'll make it. I've got to make it." She turned away from him and again tried to mount her horse. Guthrie felt a stir of male exasperation. He caught her arm and held it tightly. "Do you have any idea how far it is to Cheyenne? Do you know the way?"

She fought free almost frantically. "I don't care how far it is!" she screamed. "I'll find the way! Just let me alone, will you?"

"No, I won't. Be damned if I will. You wouldn't get five miles from town before that spooky horse'd throw you. He ain't a ladies' horse, anyhow. Where'd you get him?"

"From Saul Hubner's stable."

Guthrie grinned with no particular humor. "Why, hell, ma'am, Saul keeps a stable of hot bloods. Didn't you know that?" He saw a chance to dissuade this girl from her foolhardy venture with a minimum of argument, so he said: "Get in the buggy. I'll tie that horse on behind. I'm headed out home and my wife's got two or three horses that you'll be able to ride."

The girl looked up at him, her eyes in this dim light enormous and questioning. Apparently what she saw reassured her—a genial, red-faced elderly man whose eyes held nothing but concern for her welfare. She nodded in a tired way and meekly surrendered the reins of the big horse to him.

Guthrie tied the horse on behind the buggy, wondering grimly what his wife would say to this—this bringing home a saloon girl in the middle of the night. His reflections brought a grin to his face. Hell, she'd be so damned flabbergasted she likely wouldn't be able to say anything. Still grinning, he climbed up beside the girl, who seemed inordinately small in comparison to his own ample bulk.

He pulled up a heavy buffalo robe and tucked it carefully around her. He clucked to the buggy horse and drove out onto the long road north. Beside him, the girl snuggled deeper into the warmth of the robe. Her breathing, so fast and shallow, gradually quieted.

In silence, Guthrie drove up the long grade, bucking wind and snow all the way. Three miles from the Spur ranch house, the road wound into a deep, wide draw. In switchbacks it descended, and in switchbacks ascended the other side. In spots, the road was only a shelf blasted out of soft sandstone. All the way, it allowed passage for only one vehicle, and at the bottom of the draw, crossing Horse Thief Creek, the road became a shallow ford.

As Guthrie topped the ridge and started down the long grade, he heard the bawling of cattle—not isolated, individual moans and bellows, but rather the low, sustained bawl of many cattle in protest against being moved. A rank suspicion gripped Guthrie. What better time for rustling than a blinding blizzard? What better time for rustlers to be abroad, secure in the knowledge that the men who might stop them were snug and warm in a tight log bunkhouse?

He forgot the girl beside him, forgot everything in his righteous anger. Damn, but they were getting nervy since Zulke's acquittal! Pretty soon they'd be stealing a man's stock right out of his corral! He slapped the buggy horse's back with the reins, but he made no other noise. He drew his Colt and laid it on his lap.

The buggy slipped and slid down the narrow road, at times coming dangerously close to the brink. But each time, miraculously, it righted itself and went on. The horse's hoofs slid in the snow on the steep grade, leaving long grooves behind. The bawling of cattle drew closer. Now Guthrie could hear the *slap* of quirt on chaps, the whistles of the drovers, their shouts and curses.

Near the bottom, the road leveled momentarily and ran for a short distance almost parallel to the stream's course. And there Guthrie caught his first glimpse of the undulating movement of cattle, the lumped shapes of men in the saddle behind them. Anger stole all caution, all reason from him. A yell broke from his lips. The girl sat up in her seat with an involuntary gasp of fright.

Guthrie spoke one word to her—"Rustlers!"—and, as he did, a shout of discovery lifted from the streambed.

Most of the cattle had passed the point where the road forded the creek. As the drag stragglers rumbled away, Guthrie turned the buggy toward the ford. And then he found himself face to face with three men on horseback. Too dark for recognition— but not too dark for the sudden realization that he had let anger override reason. With sudden, paralyzing fear, Guthrie knew he was about to pay for his foolhardiness.

He yanked the gun from his lap, leveled it at a blurred shape before him, and pulled the trigger. The flash was blinding, and, coming so unexpectedly, it completely terrified both the buggy horse and the led horse. Both animals reared and the led horse broke away. Guthrie stood in the buggy, forgetting his gun, clutching the reins, hauling back on them, senselessly denying the horse its chance to drop its forehoofs to the ground. The buggy hung motionlessly, its shafts high in the air, the horse pawing at thin air. Beth screamed. And in that instant, a rustler's gun blasted.

The horse dropped as the reins relaxed. It whirled in utter terror. Then, taking the narrow, ascending road it had just descended, the animal broke into a wild run. Guthrie had fallen backward, his upper body covering the pile of packages behind the seat. The buggy careened crazily behind the frantic horse, lurching from side to side, narrowly missing the brink with each drunken lurch.

Dazedly Beth snatched the reins from Guthrie's inert grasp, tightened them, and began to drive. Having slept so long, she had no idea where she was. Having been groggy with sleep when the horse reared and whirled, she did not even know he had whirled. So she drove away from Spur with a dead man beside her, thinking all the while that she was driving toward it. And she was sick with horror at the memory her mind dredged up. For she had recognized a shouting voice in that milling trio.

A voice well known, well remembered. The voice of Russ Conover.

Behind the buggy, Russ Conover cursed bitterly, the cattle forgotten. Ernie Cassel shouted: "There was a woman in that buggy! I heard her scream!"

"An' Guthrie might not be dead," Ramon Jiminez said. "Let's go after . . . !"

"Shut up!" Conover barked. "Guthrie's dead all right!"

"How the hell do you know?"

Conover said disgustedly: "I shot him. I hit him smack in the chest. He was a still target there for a minute. Hell, you saw the way the reins went slack, didn't you?"

Cassel's voice rose with something close to hysteria. "Just the same, I'm going after them. I ain't taking no damned chances. I'm going to make sure Guthrie's dead."

"And what about the woman?" Conover snarled. "You going to kill her, too?"

"Woman?" Cassel panted, frantic. "I ain't going to leave her around to say who did this."

Conover said pityingly: "It was dark, you fool. She didn't see anything."

Cassel turned his horse. He squinted across a six-foot space at Conover. He said: "The snow makes some light. I can see you all right. I could recognize you at this distance, and she could recognize us."

Ramon whispered: "Was it Guthrie's wife?"

"I don't know how the hell it could have been," Cassel replied. "Guthrie was alone in town. I saw him a couple of times, once down at Whaite's Mercantile and once in the hotel dining room. A man might go to the store without his wife, but I'll be damned if he'd eat without her. I wouldn't anyway."

Ramon's violent shaking was visible to Conover, even in this nearly complete darkness, even at a distance of almost ten feet.

"What are we going to do?" Ramon quavered.

Conover was silent, preoccupied. A hundred yards away, obscured by the storm, the cattle stopped and began to disperse, their rumps to the wind.

"What are we going to do?" Ramon repeated.

Cassel jerked spasmodically in his saddle. He said, his voice suddenly vicious: "I know what I'm going to do, and it ain't stretching no damned rope for this night's work. I'm going to follow that buggy and make sure there's nobody going to point the finger at me."

Conover hardly heard him. He was wondering about that scream, about that woman's white, hooded face. Why did both strike such a responsive chord in his memory?

Cassel turned his horse and started away.

Conover reached out and grasped his bridle in an iron grip. "You yellow-bellied rat," he said between clenched teeth. "You follow that buggy and I'll kill you myself. We're all going home and go to bed."

All at once, Ernie Cassel became meek and submissive. It was better to risk an obscure chance of hanging later than face immediate, sure death at the hands of a Conover turned savage. He muttered: "Hell, I didn't mean it, Russ. Forget it. Let's get the hell away from here and go on home."

He sounded sincere enough, but Russ did not trust him. He accompanied Cassel home, and then, sitting his horse a quarter mile from the house, he waited until the light flickered out.

Riding toward his own home, he felt no compunction about letting Manette down. Manette had expected him to rouse Spur's crew by driving the cattle close to the house, or at least to leave a trail for them to follow in the morning. But Conover had no intention of putting his head in a noose. To hell with Manette. From tonight on it would be every man for himself.

XIV

For a while, Beth let the horse run. The animal seemed too ter-rified to slacken his pace, so Beth simply held the reins and drove. Because her excursions out of Antelope Junction never took her far from town, she was not familiar with the roads, and tonight she had no sense of direction at all. The long ride, asleep under the buffalo robe, had completely confused her regarding the distance they had covered, so she expected at any instant to drive into the sanctuary of Spur.

As the horse ran, he tired. Once he began to stumble, Beth could have stopped him with a firm drag on the reins. But she made no effort to stop him, reasoning that he would stop when fatigue forced him to. So the tiring horse ran on, and inevitably took a turn in the road too sharply. The right wheel dropped into a washout at the side of the road and the buggy leaped high into the air, very nearly overturning. It came down once against its limber springs, and then it leaped even higher into the air. This time the right wheel left the ground.

Taken unaware, Beth was thrown off the seat into the road. The wheel passed within an inch of her body. A couple of loose packages landed beside her. Then the buggy went on toward Antelope Junction.

At first, Beth lay still, stunned and unable to move. Later, upon trying to rise, she discovered that the buffalo robe was still closely wrapped about her legs and feet. Alone in this blinding, bitter storm, Beth knew a consuming despair. She would freeze to death. They would find her body when the storm ended, stiff and drifted over with snow.

Yet even in Beth, who believed she had little to live for, the instinct for self-preservation was strong. Without the strength to walk, she lay down beside the road, but she didn't just give up. That will to live made her wrap the buffalo robe tightly around her, fold after fold. Gradually drowsiness overcame her. And at last she slept.

Not far away, Roan Childress rode silently behind Otto Zulke's raiding party. His head was half buried in the turned-up collar of his sheepskin. His hat, pulled low over his eyes, warded off only a portion of the head-on blast. He had to squint against the driving snow. But always he could hear the voices and movements of Zulke's rustlers.

He dozed and his horse moved closer. He wakened and dropped back again. He would have to watch that. The horse heard the men ahead, too, and smelled their horses. Its instinct was to join forces with the others, so he would have to watch this dozing business. He sat straighter in the saddle and raised his face out of his sheepskin's collar, raised it until the icy wind beat directly into it. More uncomfortable, this, but safer.

Minutes dragged into hours. At 4:00 in the morning, he heard Zulke's bellow and saw the bright flicker of a fire in the darkness ahead. Zulke's men crowded around the fire, which was tended by two others who had been sent ahead earlier to continue drifting this herd northward.

Roan heard Zulke's query: "Where'n hell are they?"

And another man's voice: "No'th, mebbe two, three miles. They're all huddled under a bluff against this here storm."

"How many?"

"Why, now, we ain't tallied exactly. Four, five hundred mebbe."

"All right," Zulke said irritably. "Let's get moving. We ain't got all night."

Roan saw Zulke scatter the embers of the fire with his boot. Then the rustlers moved on, riding more swiftly now.

Roan kept his distance, but being downwind from the rustlers, he had no trouble following their conversation. The drawling voice that had spoken back at the fire spoke again:

"Where you-all takin' these here critters?"

Zulke laughed shortly. "Not you-all. Us-all, brother. You're goin' along."

"Shore. But where we headin'?"

"The Yellowstone. There's winter feed for 'em in the hot-springs meadows up there, an' there's not likely to be anybody passin' through there this time of year. We'll change the brands and stick around until they're healed. At least three or four of us will. The rest can go back."

"Who's goin' back?"

"Why, the men that's got wives an' kids, I expect. Christmas is only four days off."

Roan heard grumbling then, low-voiced cursing, and a rueful remark: "Damn! That lets me out. An' I promised a little ole gal in Antelope Junction that I'd. . . ."

Zulke laughed. "Plenty of single men around town on Christmas. She ain't goin' to miss you."

Then a ribald chorus of laughter.

A bluff loomed up. The dark red shape of a cow appeared on Roan's right, and he hauled back on his reins abruptly. He heard Zulke call: "Here they are! Gather 'em up, boys."

Roan started to turn his horse. He saw the shape of a horseman coming at him out of the gloom ahead, and leaned forward to clamp his hand over his horse's nostrils. He was too late. The horse, smelling and seeing another and having been alone so long, loosed a shrill, high whinny. Roan flipped up the skirt of his coat, uncovering his gun. The man, who might have gone by him, unseeing in the darkness, now halted, and called with plain surprise: "What the hell? Who's that?"

Roan considered answering, trying to bluff this out. As abruptly as the thought came to him, he rejected it. He'd never make it stick. This man must have peeled off from the others as Zulke spoke, and would know that no one else could have beat him here. The surprise, the unbelief in his voice told Roan that. With no other course open to him, Roan sank spurs into his horse's sides, wheeling him as he spurred. Behind him, a shot rang out, flat and muffled by the snow. Roan lay low on his horse's neck, merciless with his spurs, careless of arroyos, deadfalls, and rocks that might lie in his path. He galloped into the night with the alarmed shouts of the rustlers still ringing in his ears.

XV

Childress rode with a frantic haste, but he wasn't entirely concerned with his own safety. Rustlers or not, he liked some of the men behind him and he didn't want to shoot at them. Nor was he sure, right now, whether he would turn over their names to Houston. For he was beginning to see this whole sordid mess in the way it really deserved to be seen. Neither side could be called entirely wrong, neither side entirely right. Here in Corbin County, rich men and poor men alike were simply doing what their hearts told them was right or necessary.

Rustlers? Of course these settlers were rustlers. But they were not stealing for personal gain. They were retaliating for a wrong, in the only way they knew. Nor could Childress entirely blame the larger ranchers. They had, in many cases, bought and paid for more land than they had received. And so they had set out to remedy the shortage in their own direct way, a way that was as much a product of their character development as the settlers' way was a product of theirs. Even as he raced away from the yelling death at his heels, Roan felt sick, shamed. For money, he had come in here to spy upon and betray the settlers, among whom he now lived and worked. In justice to himself, he admitted that, if he had known the situation earlier, he would never have taken the job. But the thought gave him little comfort.

An arroyo yawned before him, and his horse lifted suddenly

over it. A clump of jack pine made a blob of darkness on his right. His horse slid, and recovered on an expanse of bare, flat rock.

Gradually the sounds of pursuit faded from behind him. The settlers must have realized they could never run him down in such a storm. They'd slowed up and begun to track. They would split up, Roan knew. There were eight of them altogether. Eight—but they would need at least four to complete the cattle drive to the Yellowstone. So they might spare four to chase him. In fact, they almost had to spare four, because they could not afford to let him escape.

He weighed his chances of escape and found them poor. Only by great speed could he hope to outdistance them enough so that the wind and snow would obscure his trail. So he drove his horse mercilessly, knowing that his life depended on the tired animal. And he asked himself this question, needing its answer desperately before the time came to face his pursuers: *Will you fight back?* With sinking heart, he knew he would not.

Dawn found him still free. But his horse's head hung spiritlessly, and the animal was lathered and hot. Roan climbed to a rock bluff and gazed bleakly northward over his back trail. Gradually, in the last couple of hours, he had been bearing west, in the hope that, if the rustlers had lost his trail, they would go on by him, thinking he was heading for Antelope Junction.

The snow still fell, but not as hard as before. The wind had diminished until it was but a stiff breeze. Roan could see a long way out across the rolling, hilly plain. He saw the four at the very rim of his vision, moving like specks across the frozen wastes. He watched them for a full five minutes, determining their direction, determining also that they were not following him. They had indeed lost his trail.

He knew he had not been recognized. If he could get into

town, he would be safe. But not on a played out, lathered horse. There would be no explanation for that. He thought of Jerome Guthrie's Spur Ranch, which lay eastward, a few miles north of town. He could explain to Guthrie his connection with Houston, and quite possibly the man would be able to give him a horse that didn't bear the Spur brand.

He led his horse back out of sight behind the bluff, unsaddled, and rubbed him down, then tied him to a tree. He spread his blanket on the lee side of a huge rock, lay down, and promptly went to sleep.

When he awoke, the sun was above the horizon and trying hard to poke a hole in the clouds. Roan sprang to his feet, surprised at the length of time he had slept. He found his horse, saddled, and swung onto the animal's back. The night had taken a heavy toll of the horse. His head drooped and he plodded along without spirit.

Roan struck the road a couple of miles from Spur and turned northward with a somewhat wistful glance over his shoulder in the direction of town. He had never been this hungry in his life, nor quite as anxious to sit down before a hot cup of coffee.

He rounded a turn, then, and came upon Beth MacPherson, sitting by the side of the road wrapped in an enormous buffalo robe. He pulled up. A certain blankness in her eyes told him instantly that something was very much amiss.

He was careful to dismount slowly, careful not to approach her at once. He squatted down ten feet from her and fished in his pocket for makings. He rolled a cigarette and lighted it before he spoke. Then he said, as though it were an everyday occurrence for him to meet a woman under these unusual circumstances: "Hello, Beth. How are you?"

Her face was white, strained, and taut. Roan supposed she had not yet recovered from her hysterics in the Custer the night before—or that the shock had impaired her reason. She nodded mutely.

"How did you get this far from town, Beth? Did you walk out here?" He studied her closely, wondering if she were frostbitten. He doubted it, for she seemed adequately covered by the buffalo robe, and he knew of nothing warmer. An expression of pain twisted her face briefly, pain that Roan guessed instinctively was born in her mind rather than in her body. He asked softly: "Has something else happened, Beth? Tell me, did you walk out here?"

"No. I rode out . . . in a buggy."

"Who did you ride with, Beth?"

"I don't know. I don't know who he was."

Roan edged a little closer, but stopped as her eyes widened. "What happened, Beth?"

"There was shooting." She spoke as though in a daze.

"The shooting was back in town, Beth."

"No. There was more shooting. The horse ran away. The man was dead and I had to drive." She covered her face with her hands. Her shoulders shook but she did not cry.

"How did you get here?"

"I was thrown out of the buggy."

Roan had a sinking feeling. A man in a buggy almost certainly meant one of the large ranchers, since he doubted if any of the settlers even owned a buggy. On this road, it almost certainly meant Jerome Guthrie, owner of Spur. He tried to keep his fears from showing in his face.

"How would you like to ride my horse?" he asked.

She showed no interest.

Roan said: "You can't stay here, Beth. Aren't you cold, and hungry? Wouldn't you like some hot coffee?"

She gave him a very small, very timid smile.

Roan said heartily: "Fine. Let me help you up. You ride my

horse and I'll lead him. In a little while we'll be where it's warm and where there will be something to eat."

He helped her to her feet, boosted her up on his weary horse, and managed to tuck the robe about her so that it would stay.

He said: "Hold onto the saddle horn, Beth. I won't go fast."

She did, with both hands, like a good child, and Roan stepped out toward Spur, leading his horse.

It seemed a long time before he came into the yard. He noticed that the bunkhouse chimney was cold, that the door hung ajar as though the crew had left in a hurry. The corral was almost empty.

Roan hesitated, but finally, hearing a sound from the direction of the house, he dismounted and walked that way. Leaving Beth sitting quietly on the ground-tied horse, he climbed the three wide steps to the verandah and knocked on the door.

After what seemed an interminable time, the door opened. A woman stood in the doorway, her face streaked and haggard with tears, her eyes red yet brimming. She said with a catch in her voice: "Yes?"

"Missus Guthrie? I'm Roan Childress. I'm working for Colonel Houston, although we don't want it known just yet. I have a girl with me that I found beside the road, and I need a horse."

Her eyes turned suspicious as he had feared they would. Roan noticed two healthy, red-faced boys behind her. He guessed their ages at somewhere near nine and five. They had been crying, too, and they stared at Roan with plain dislike.

Roan guessed what the trouble was but he had to be sure. He asked: "Is something the matter, ma'am?"

"My husband has been killed." A sob caught in her throat and she brought a fine lace handkerchief to her mouth. She made a visible fight for control, won, and looked straight at Roan. "There are horses in the corral. Help yourself, Mister

Childress. I'll tell Hank Blayne, the foreman, that you have them."

"I thought," Roan said, "maybe you might. . . ." He shook his head. "No. You have troubles enough of your own."

"What did you think, Mister Childress?"

"This girl . . . she's a singer at the Custer Saloon . . . has had a bad shock. Two of them in fact, because she saw your husband killed. I thought maybe you'd let her stay here until she's warm and rested. She spent the night alone out in the storm."

Mrs. Guthrie's face had not shown any particular change when Roan mentioned that Beth sang in the saloon. Now she left the door and went down off the verandah. Looking up at Beth, she asked: "What's your name, my dear?"

"Beth."

"Would you like something to eat?"

Beth nodded. Roan stepped over and helped her from the saddle. Mrs. Guthrie said to Roan: "You go on. I'll look after her, poor child."

From the doorway, one of the boys piped: "Who's that, Mom? Who's the lady?"

"Never mind. But she's going to stay with us a while."

For an instant, Roan felt eternally proud of the human race. He said—"Thanks, Missus Guthrie."—and walked toward the corral.

He felt a mounting anger because Guthrie should never have died, because this woman should never have been widowed, or her sons deprived of their father. But the anger could find no easy outlet, because in a sense Guthrie had brought this on himself. What good would it do to tell Mrs. Guthrie that there was right on the side of her husband's killers? Would that comfort her in her loss? Would it help her to say that Guthrie had been greedy, that he had taken grassland by force, grassland to which he had no legal or moral right? No. The crimes men committed were still crimes, no matter how just or understandable the reasons for their commission.

Scowling, Roan roped a big unbranded gray out of the small bunch in the corral. He transferred his saddle from his own horse, and led the tired animal to the water trough. He chopped a hole in the ice so the horse could drink, then turned him into the corral.

A long manger ran along one side of·the corral, and it was filled with hay. Roan's horse lay down in the snow, rolled, then got up, and began to eat.

Roan went back to the gray, bridled him, then stood thinking while he coiled his rope. He had been reluctant to turn over his list of rustlers to Houston. Now it seemed unavoidable. The list certainly included the name of Guthrie's killer, and he must be brought to justice. By hauling them into court, the men who had been with Guthrie's killer last night could be made to talk. It was the only way. Childress mounted the borrowed gray horse and set out at a steady lope toward Antelope Junction.

To a casual observer, Antelope Junction might have appeared peaceful, normal, even sleepy. To Roan Childress, riding in just before noon, it was a town on the brink of war.

Down in front of the Custer Saloon a group of settlers argued in low, impassioned tones. On the hotel verandah, Colonel Houston took his stand, backed by the battered, beaten, but still poisonous Ransom Coates and half a dozen of his hardcase crew.

Gustav Orr walked the street between the two groups, trying to appear calm and unconcerned, but eloquently revealing his mounting anxiety in the quick, nervous glances he threw at both groups. Roan felt a stir of pity for the man. It was not that Orr was a coward. A coward would not be here now, standing between the match and the powder keg, making a buffer of himself. But Orr lacked the stature, the force of will to cope with this explosive situation. Orr would live only so long as it suited both factions to let him live. He was the settlers' sheriff, and from them he expected the greatest tolerance. Yet if he tried to take a murderer from among their ranks—a thing that Houston would surely demand—then he would instantly lose the settlers' support. Roan didn't envy him his job.

But Roan had something to face, too, this morning—Ransom Coates's pale yellow eyes, which picked him up at the edge of town and followed him to the hotel hitching rail.

Dismounting with his horse between him and Coates, Roan unbuttoned his coat and loosened his gun in its holster.

Down before the Custer Saloon, the settlers saw this movement, and stirred uneasily. Someone in that group said something, and almost as one0 they stepped into the street and began their slow advance toward the Teton Hotel.

Roan knew what the consequences would be if the settlers entered his quarrel with Coates. In one word—carnage. He gave a low, soft curse, touched by their unhesitating and wordless offer of support, shamed because he did not deserve it. He came around his horse's head and took the hotel steps in a couple of bounds.

Coates stepped back, surprised. Only surprise held off his grab for the gun at his thigh. Roan said—"Houston, watch your boy."—in a loud, clear voice, and added in an urgent whisper: "I want to see you."

Then he was past the group, and standing in the hotel lobby.

Close. Too damned close. Roan discovered that he was sweating, that his hands, usually so steady under stress, were shaking. The man at the desk, frankly scared, stared at him as he crossed the lobby and climbed the stairs. Roan went unhesitatingly down the hall and, without knocking, opened the door that led to Houston's quarters. Then he sat down on the horsehair sofa and waited.

XVI

He did not have to wait long. He heard steps in the uncarpeted hotel hallway, and the door flung open behind him. He fished his sack of Durham from his pocket and carefully built himself a wheat-straw cigarette. Not until he lighted it did he turn on the sofa and look up at Houston.

Red-faced and angry, the colonel stood, spraddle-legged, glaring. "You said you wanted to see me."

The arrogant, almost contemptuous tone sawed on Roan's nerves, but he got lazily to his feet. He said: "Damn you, Houston, don't use that Army snarl on me."

Veins popped out and throbbed on Houston's florid forehead. He reminded Roan of a firecracker with a sputtering fuse.

Something about Roan's eyes put out the fuse. Houston said throatily: "You wanted to see me. Do you have the list?"

"I have it," Roan said. "There's a question or two, though."

"Question? Question? Who the hell are you to question me?" Houston moved away from the door and stalked furiously into the center of the room.

Roan fished a small canvas sack from his trousers pocket. He held it in the palm of his left hand while his right fumbled in a shirt pocket and came out with a folded sheet of paper. He said: "I've got the six hundred you paid me here in this canvas sack. I've got the list you want in the other hand. You're going to get one or the other . . . but I haven't decided yet which it's going to be."

He thought the bulging blood vessels in Houston's forehead were going to burst. The man was speechless. Then, very slowly, the color ebbed from Houston's face. The pounding veins subsided. The eyes lost their raging intensity and turned cold and hard. The man's thin lips made a tight, humorless smile.

"What do you want to know?" Houston asked.

A lifetime of rigid self-discipline had made Houston's recovery possible, a lifetime of Army training. Roan felt a stir of reluctant respect. He said: "That's better."

"What do you want to know?"

"There's a name on this list that you would like to have. Orr would like to have it, too. It's the name of Guthrie's murderer."

"You know who he is?"

"I don't know who he is, but I know he's on this list. What I would like to be told is how you propose to find out who he is. And I would like to know what you expect to do with the rest of the names. You can't prosecute in Corbin County or it will be a Zulke case all over again. They'll be acquitted. I want to know what you're going to do."

"I don't think that's any of your business. You were paid to get the names and the evidence."

"And I got them. I'll tell you something, Colonel, something you don't know. You lost five hundred head of cattle last night, and Guthrie lost a like amount. You think you broke up their raids, don't you? Your crews came in this morning and told you they'd discovered a raid and broken it up, didn't they? Well, they were wrong. The raids that were broken up and the raid that resulted in Guthrie's death were fake raids, planned to draw your attention from the big steal going on up north."

Roan watched the effect of his information on Houston. The man's mouth fell open and his eyes mirrored his utter unbelief. But only for an instant, for he must have seen that Roan was telling the truth. He finally found his voice: "Man, give me that list. Maybe I can't convict them in Corbin County. Maybe I can't convict them in any court in Wyoming. But they'll pay. There's a way of handling renegades and thieves that's worked very well before. And it'll work again! Give me that list." He stretched out a hand and advanced toward Roan.

Roan took a couple of quick backward steps. His right hand returned the list to his pocket and dropped to the grips of his gun. He tossed the canvas sack at Houston's feet.

"You've told me what I needed to know, Colonel. You don't get the list. You get your money back. Do you think I'd turn over the names of these men to you, knowing you intended to murder them? You underestimate me, Colonel."

With his hand lightly on the butt of his gun, he backed toward the door. He said: "We're square, Colonel. You got your money back, and I got back my self-respect."

His left hand went out behind him, reaching for the knob of the door. He kept on watching the colonel's face, for there was wildness in it, wildness beyond control. His decision had spelled the colonel's defeat, and defeat was a thing he could not stand.

Roan fumbled for the doorknob and his hand encountered only empty space. He saw the colonel's eyes flicker, saw the sick glare of defeat become a bright gleam of triumph. In that instant, Roan knew he had lost. He heard, rather than felt, the gun barrel strike his skull. Then lights flashed before his eyes and the world went black.

XVII

Gustav Orr heaved a long, slow sigh as he saw Colonel Houston whirl after Roan Childress on the hotel verandah. Tension went out of him with a rush as Ransom Coates followed like an elongated shadow of the older man.

Standing there in the dismal, cold street, Orr had an inward look at himself and was ashamed at what he saw. Yet this very shame made his stance stern and straight as the group of settlers approached, and put a new timbre of command in his voice as he said: "Get out of town, the bunch of you! How the hell do you expect a man to keep the peace with you hanging around the front of the Custer like a bunch of stray dogs?"

Conover, in the vanguard of the settlers, tossed his head in the direction of Houston's crew, still lounging defiantly on the hotel verandah. "How about them, Orr? You going to run them out of town, too?" Conover, Orr could see, had been emboldened by the departure of Coates. Conover feared the tall, deadly gunman, and, truthfully, Orr couldn't blame him.

The sheriff said: "You wouldn't be telling me how to run my business, would you, Russ?"

"Maybe you need someone to tell you," Russ said, but something about his defiance wasn't right. He sounded scared. He acted scared.

Orr said: "Conover, where were you last night?" Conover was a man of medium height, bulky of shoulder and thick of chest. He had the lean hips of a saddle man and he dressed range fashion in woolly chaps and heavy sheepskin coat.

He scowled blackly at the question. "I was home in bed," he said. "Where the hell else would I be? Are you asking that question of every man you see, or did you single me out? Tell me that, Orr."

Orr studied Conover, who met the scrutiny without flinching. Orr's eyes dropped away first. He decided that he had been wrong. Conover wasn't scared—not any more than a lot of men around this town today. He wasn't any more scared than Orr was himself.

The sheriff grunted: "All right, Conover." He fixed the group with his blue-eyed stare. "Damn it, the bunch of you have got to start using some sense. Zulke proved that rustling was a good business in Corbin County. But don't crowd your luck. Don't push it too far. Don't make the mistake of thinking that just because I'll shut my eyes to a little rustling, I'll do the same for murder. Because you're wrong, boys. Dead wrong."

Feet shuffled in the snow underfoot. Someone growled: "Nobody asked you to wink at murder, Sheriff."

And another said: "I'm going home. I've got more to do than hang around town all day."

It was what Orr wanted, but he watched them go with little satisfaction. A temporary stopgap, this. Clear the town of the opposing factions and hope to avoid bloodshed. He smiled a little, grimly. That was like the ostrich, shoving his head into the sand so he couldn't see approaching danger. He made a lonely, forlorn figure there in the broad street. Just the same, he straightened up and tilted his hat slightly forward. Then he walked across toward the hotel verandah to order Houston's crew out of town. Surprisingly Orr encountered no resistance from Houston's crew. They talked it over briefly, and then rode out of town in a body.

That puzzled Orr. Still, a man ought to be able to expect some breaks. All of his luck hadn't ought to be bad. Relieved, Orr stamped across the street, turned off Main, and entered his office on the first floor of the courthouse. Immediately after the buggy bearing Guthrie's body reached town, Orr had taken a couple of deputies and ridden out to Horse Thief Creek to look at the ground, and had sent a man to inform Mrs. Guthrie of her husband's death, taking a short cut across country. He had expected to find nothing, and he had found nothing. Heavy snow, drifting during the night, completely obliterated both the rustlers' tracks and the tracks of the buggy.

Now he kicked the problem around in his mind. This morning he had received reports of rustling not only from Houston's, but also from the foremen of three other large ranches. That meant one thing. The settlers had thrown away all caution and made their big bid. Orr thought: *I ought to see Manette. Maybe he can talk some sense into them.*

He got up and put on his hat. He stepped out into the courthouse corridor and inserted the key into his office door, locking it. He paid no particular attention when he heard the outside door open, but he whirled nervously as Houston's arrogant voice said: "Unlock it, Sheriff. I want to talk to you."

Orr shrugged and inclined his head. Resignedly he unlocked the door and swung it open.

Houston stalked into the sheriff's office. He carried a sort of short riding crop that he kept tapping impatiently against his solid thigh.

"A hell of a sheriff you are," Houston said. "Do you know that I lost five hundred head last night . . . that Guthrie lost the same amount? The raids you've been hearing about all morning were dummy raids to cover the big steal going on up north."

Orr had a sinking, sickish sensation in his stomach. He was like a fire watcher in a forest who has just seen a creeping ground blaze leap to the crowns of the trees and race over his head. He felt surrounded, enveloped, ready to be devoured. He said: "What do you want me to do, Colonel Houston?"

"Do? Do? Not a damned thing, Orr. From here on out, I'll handle it all by myself. Only keep your nose out of it or you're going to get hurt. Is that clear enough?"

"Don't use that tone on me, Colonel." He said the words, and there ought to have been anger in them, but they sounded hollow. They were only a defeated man's feeble protest.

"I'll use any damned tone I please. Stay out of my way, Orr. Stay out of it or stop lead. It's just that simple." He stood there, tapping the crop against his knee, staring at Orr with his stony eyes. He might have faced an insubordinate, drunk, and disorderly trooper in just this way, and his manner beat Orr's spirit to the ground.

The colonel whirled and strutted out of the office like a victorious bantam rooster. Orr sank into his swivel chair and dropped his head into his hands.

For a long while he sat huddled thus. But gradually an idea was born in his mind. Colonel Houston had made Orr think of the Army. Orr knew the law. Orr was the duly constituted law in Corbin County. He could appeal to the United States Army for help. It was the only dim ray of light in an otherwise black picture. Orr reached into a cubbyhole in his desk and pulled out a sheet of writing paper. Picking up a pen, he dipped it into his inkwell and began to write.

Janet Houston had heard Roan Childress as he entered the sitting room, but she paid no particular attention, thinking it was her father. She was mending a rip in one of her gowns, sitting beside the bedroom window in a *creaking* rocker. She heard the door open and close a second time, then heard her father's sharp voice. She stopped mending, her hands idle and oddly tense in her lap.

A tremor ran through her as she caught the even cadences of Roan Childress's deep voice. She could not hear their words, but she sensed some kind of quarrel. Shamelessly she laid aside her mending, walked quietly to the door, and put her ear against its thin panel.

Except for the opening sentence or two, she heard the quarrel in its entirety. She heard the gun barrel *thud* on Roan's head, and Ransom Coates's ugly laugh.

She flung the door open. "That was a cowardly thing!"

Houston looked quickly at her, then back at Coates. He said: "Get out of here, Ransom. I'll talk to you later."

Coates scowled at Houston. He opened his mouth to speak, then changed his mind. With a surly grunt, he opened the door and disappeared into the hall.

Janet crossed the room and peered outside. Coates was walking toward the stairs. She felt an odd and puzzling stir of revulsion, looking at his back, almost the same feeling she had when she saw a snake cross the road in summer.

She turned, closing the door behind her. She discovered that she was trembling. She looked at Roan Childress, big and limp on the floor. A blood trickle ran from his hair onto the carpet. She knelt, picked up his wrist, and felt his pulse.

"Help me get him onto the sofa," she said, and her voice had a quality that halted the colonel's protest.

Roan's body was heavy. But between them, panting and tugging, they managed to lift him, one end at a time, onto the lumpy sofa. Breathing hard, Houston muttered an excuse and hurried out of the room.

That did nothing to lessen Janet's ire. She wanted to have this out with him, now, while she was still furious enough to speak without fear. Yet she knew it was better for Houston to leave. Not only did Roan need attention, but she might say things to her father that were better left unsaid.

She got a towel from the washstand and dipped an end of it into the pitcher of cold water. Then she returned to Roan and bathed the nasty lump on his head. The scalp was deeply gashed for almost two inches and bleeding freely. His pulse was slow, too. Janet washed the blood away, then mopped his face with the cold water. He did not stir.

Janet got up and went out into the hall. From the head of the stairs, she called to the clerk: "Mister Adams! Would you get Doctor Graves for me, please?"

"Sure, Miss Houston. You sick?"

"No. A man has been hurt. Hurry."

She returned to the room, pulled a chair over beside the sofa, and sat down. She had done all she could for Childress, but he might have a concussion, or even a fractured skull. Ransom Coates must have put unnecessary force into this blow because he hated Childress.

She stared at Childress pensively, very much aware of the attraction he had for her. There was an odd boyishness about him, lying unconscious there, a quality he didn't possess when awake. She smiled as she studied him.

He could not be called a handsome man. He was much too rugged to match any conventional standards for handsomeness. And he was all man. He left no doubt as to that. His appearance shouted it, and so did his actions. Janet could not remember any single man in Corbin County, save her father who employed him, who had dared to cross Ransom Coates since his arrival three years before. But Childress had. He had beaten Coates twice, and he seemed indifferent to Coates's threats. Watching Childress lying there, a coldness crept slowly through Janet's body, the coldness of fear and foreboding.

Dr. Graves came and in his cool, preoccupied way painted the gash on Childress's head, stitched it closed with catgut, and applied a bandage. Childress was stirring as he finished, groaning softly. His eyes opened, looked at the doctor, and then at Janet. He struggled to sit up. His hand went to his shirt pocket, and came away.

Graves put a hand on his chest and held him down. "Young man," he said briskly, "you should have a fractured skull, but you only have a mild concussion. Don't get up just yet or you'll fall on your face." He straightened and closed his black bag with a snap. "Keep him on his back a while, Miss Houston. Shall I send my bill to the colonel?"

Roan stirred, groping toward his pants pocket, but Janet said, smiling: "Yes. Send your bill to the colonel."

After the doctor left, Roan said: "It's gone. The list is gone."

"I know. I heard the whole thing. I was in my bedroom all the time."

"Do you know what he intends doing with that list?"

"He'll turn it over to the sheriff, I suppose."

"No. Orr will never see it. Your father intends to loose Coates and a few more like him on the country. They'll go down that list a name at a time, until. . . ."

Janet stood up, suddenly pale. "Mister Childress, I won't listen to that kind of talk. My father is a law-abiding man, not a murderer."

Childress shrugged, and smiled, and seemed to concede the point. He swung his legs off the sofa and sat up. He dropped his head into his hands and sat utterly motionless for a few moments. With his head still in his hands, he said softly: "Tell me about your father, Miss Houston. What is he like? What has he been? What has he done?"

Janet thought it odd, this curiosity concerning a man who had been responsible for that nasty blow on Childress's head no more than half an hour ago. But Janet had heard that people were not always completely rational for a while following even a mild concussion. She thought it best to humor Roan, and, besides, she wanted to talk to him. She felt almost as though she had known Roan a lifetime. He seemed so calm, so sure.

"My father is a strange man," she said slowly. "He has no real friends. But his employees are loyal to him." She smiled. "When I was a child, just after mother died, he was very good to me. He would tuck me into my bed at night, and then sit on its edge and tell me stories."

"What kind of stories?"

"Oh, stories about his Army life, about Indian battles, about the Civil War. He served with the first Colorado Volunteers at Apache Cañon, and later with Colonel Chivington at. . . ."

"The battle of Sand Creek?"

"Why, yes. How did you know?"

"I didn't know. I guessed." She sensed an odd intensity in him now. "How did he feel about that battle, Miss Houston?"

"Feel?" She remembered the exultation that always shown in her father's eyes as he told that particular tale. At first she had urged him to tell it often, for his excitement in telling it could transmit itself to her. But as she grew older, she began to know pity for the Indians, men, women and children, who had been slain that black day. Pity that the colonel didn't seem to share.

She said thoughtfully: "Telling it seemed to excite him. His eyes would almost glow." Janet shook her head to clear it of memories. "Let's talk about something else. You, for instance. Roan is an odd name. How did you get it?"

In the manner of a man sharing a confidence, he said: "Full name's Roanoke. Name of a family plantation in North Carolina. The family left it at about the time I was born. I suppose they named me after it because they loved it. It was destroyed during the war."

"They were Southern people, then?"

"Yes. They came West. Settled in Montana, but the country was too hard for them. Too cold. Mother died when I was seven, my father when I was ten."

"I'm sorry."

"It's been a long time." He grinned and gingerly got to his feet. He swayed.

Janet stepped quickly toward him. She caught his arms with her two hands, meaning only to steady him. So quickly did it happen that she had no time to protest. His arms went around her, strong and hungry, and drew her close.

For an instant her face was buried against his chest. Then slowly, her arms crept up around his neck and she raised her face for his kiss. It was firm, and strong, filled with a lonely man's yearning, and Janet answered it with equal strength, with equal warmth. It was he who drew away first, with his face set cold and harsh. He said: "I'm sorry. I had no right to do that."

"But I wanted you to. I think I've wanted you to since that first day on the courthouse steps." She smiled at him shyly. "You see, I'm a direct woman."

He swung away from her, and his voice sounded strange, pinched: "It can't come to anything. Your father took that list

145

from me and I know what he intends to do with it. I've got to stop him if I can. I owe that much to the men I turned in."

Suddenly Janet felt cheated, unreasoningly furious. She said bitterly: "Rustlers! Murderers! That's what you want to protect!"

"Men, with the faults of men," he said dully. "Men like myself, married to women like you. And kids. They've seen the range gobbled up and they're looking at a bleak future. Now they're fighting in the only way they know how." He sighed. "I would have given your father that list had he wanted it only for the purpose of legal prosecution. But I wouldn't hand over a list of victims to the executioner."

Raging, Janet rushed at him. Her hand swung viciously, and its sound against his cheek was flat and loud.

"Get out!" she said. "I never want to see you again!"

Shrugging wearily, Roan picked up his hat and walked unsteadily to the door. He went through it without looking back.

Ever honest, even with herself, Janet knew that her anger had been so terrible only because she suspected that what Roan said was true. And she knew something else, something that made her shiver. Roan would live only until such time as Ransom Coates and her father could arrange a fight, a fight that he would have no chance of winning. Yet what could she do now? What could a woman do? Warn him? He did not need warning, for he was not a fool. Try to persuade her father to let him alone? Her father would laugh at her. Shaking uncontrollably, Janet sank into a chair and dropped her face into her hands.

XVIII

Roan's head ached abominably as he slowly descended the stairs to the lobby. Objects reeled and swayed before his eyes. Crossing the lobby, he staggered and almost fell. But the cold, outside air had its reviving effect. He paused before the hotel, fished his makings from his pocket, and stared bleakly at the all but empty street while he made his cigarette. He licked the edge of the paper, touched a match to its end, and then he saw Sheriff Orr come into Main from the direction of the courthouse. Orr headed for the post office between the hotel and the Custer Saloon, and he carried a white envelope.

On impulse, Roan moved to intercept him. The sheriff paused and eyed the bandage on Roan's head. "Brawling again?" he asked sourly.

Roan grinned. "The receiving end this time. I was slugged."

Orr's expression curdled completely. "And now you want to swear out an assault complaint? Don't you think I've got anything better to do than that?"

Roan's grin lost its humor, but it did not fade. He said: "No complaint. I just want to talk to you. It might pay you to listen."

Orr shrugged. "All right. Wait till I mail this letter." Leaving Roan standing there, he walked over to the post office, went inside briefly, and then came back. "Come on over to the courthouse," he said without enthusiasm, and led the way. Roan followed, wondering at his conflicting opinions of this man. One minute he would find himself respecting the sheriff, the next glimpsing the weakness in him, the ineffectiveness.

Orr clumped into the courthouse and unlocked his door. He nodded at a straight-backed chair. "Well, what is it?" he asked testily.

"First, you ought to know what I've been doing here. Not that I'm proud of it, you understand, but you ought to know. I've been working for Houston, gathering evidence of rustling."

The sheriff's eyes widened.

"I managed to get a list of names for Houston, thinking he wanted to prosecute in the courts. When I began to suspect that was not his intention, I asked him right out what he meant to do with the list." Roan paused and carefully dropped his cigarette stub into the brass spittoon. "Houston made it pretty plain that he'd no intention of taking the men to court. That left just one way for him to handle it, and I didn't like that way. I refused to give him the list and started to back out of the room." Roan reached up and touched his bandaged head gingerly.

Orr said bleakly: "Then he's got his list now, huh? How many names were on it?"

"Damned near seventy of them. They were the ones that took part in all those raids last night."

"You know where the thousand cattle went?"

Roan nodded. "But I'm not telling."

Orr kneaded his eyes with his knuckles. "You didn't kill Weeks at all, did you?"

Roan shook his head. "I was decoyed away to an empty stable that night, supposedly to meet Houston. But Houston didn't show. My guess would be Coates on that. He was the only one with a reason for hating me. Aside from Weeks, of course."

Orr sighed. "Probably was Coates. You leaving the country now?"

"No," Roan said evenly. "I made an honest mistake, Sheriff. I didn't like what I was doing, but, hell, they were rustling. Now that I see what I've done, I don't intend to run. I'll stay and see if I can't help straighten it out."

Orr frowned. "What do you think Houston will do?"

Roan did not reply immediately. When he did, his voice was low-pitched, doubtful. "You won't believe it."

"Try me."

"Hell, I can hardly believe it myself. But you know what I think? I think Houston intends to kill every man on that list he can get, and run the rest out of the country."

He watched Orr for reaction, and he got it. Orr started violently, and then he stared at nothing for a long minute.

Finally he said: "He stood right here in this room less'n an hour ago and told me he was going to handle it himself. Told me to stay out of it or stop lead. I've been thinking the same thing you have, but it's hard to believe. It's hard to believe a man can plan anything like that. Who does he think he is? The Almighty?"

"I don't know," Roan said. "Thing is, what are you going to do about it?"

"Man, what can I do? I'm only one law officer. I've got two deputies, one of them hot-headed and the other on the stupid side. Do you think I can stop Houston with a force like that?" Roan let it lie. The sheriff scrubbed his chin, then apparently reached some decision. "I've written the commandant over at Fort McBurney and asked for help. But you know the Army. Maybe I'll get it and maybe I won't."

Roan stood up. He said—"You could fight him with a force of settlers."—but even as he said it, he knew the sheriff could not accept such a solution. It would be tantamount to declaring an open class war in Corbin County.

Orr was saying: "A man hadn't ought to have to face anything this big. He hadn't ought to have to." His voice took on an indignant tone. "I took office almost five years ago and I always figured I was big enough to be sheriff in this county. I've done my job, catching killers and bank robbers, jailing drunks, serving papers that Judge Pumphrey gives me to serve. But a sheriff hadn't ought to have to stand between two armies."

Roan said uncomfortably: "I'll go back to Manette's. If he wants me to stay after he hears what I have to tell him, then you'll find me there when you want me. Otherwise, I'll come back to town."

"All right." The sheriff seemed to have lost interest in Roan. His eyes, tortured and sunk deeply in their sockets, did not even look up. The sheriff was in some private kind of hell, and nothing Roan or anyone else could say would help him.

Roan went out the door, closing it softly behind him. And now he faced the hardest task he had faced in his life—telling Manette that he had been a spy, that he had compiled a list of men who had participated in the rustling raids, and that through stupidity he had lost possession of the list. He had to tell Manette what Houston intended to do, and how slight was the chance of stopping him. He had to hand Manette his death warrant, and those of almost seventy of his friends.

He walked across Main to the hotel hitch rail and untied the horse he had borrowed from Guthrie's Spur Ranch. Then he rode out of town toward the south.

Tolan rolled out of his blankets this morning with the oddest feeling of uneasiness he had ever known. As was his habit, he reached first for the cigarette papers and tobacco on the floor beside his bunk, made himself a cigarette, and lighted it. He and Roan had been sleeping in a small, makeshift bunkhouse that had formerly been a granary. Roan's bunk was empty and untouched.

Tolan dragged deeply on the cigarette and stared at the ceiling. Had Roan been hurt? Could be, but he hadn't waked up worrying about Roan. He threw off the blankets and sat up. Beth. That was it. Roan could take care of himself. Beth couldn't.

The room was icy cold. He pulled on his trousers fast, then slipped into his boots. He was buttoning up his shirt when he heard the *crunch* of hoofs in the yard. He did not take time to belt his gun around his waist. He snatched the weapon from its holster and stepped out of the door.

Manette was riding into the yard. His face was gray with weariness, his eyes blank and sick. Tolan jammed his gun into his belt. Manette rode up to him and dismounted.

"What's the matter?" Tolan asked.

"Hell to pay," Manette breathed wearily. "Jerome Guthrie was shot last night. And it's my fault. I was behind the raids we made on his and Houston's cattle. But . . . but how was I to know he'd blunder right into the middle of the raiders?"

Tolan said: "You didn't shoot him. Quit worrying about it. Is he dead?"

Manette nodded.

Tolan said: "You look played out. Let me take care of your horse."

"Thanks."

Manette walked dispiritedly across the yard and entered the house. Tolan headed for the barn, leading Manette's horse. He took care of the animal, then tramped through the snow to the back door. He stamped snow from his boots and went in.

Manette sat at the kitchen table, sipping a scalding cup of coffee. His wife stood over the stove, frying ham and flapjacks. Tolan took off his hat, laid it on the floor beside the door.

Conversation had stilled between Manette and his wife as Tolan entered. Manette said: "It's all right, Lilac. Tolan knows."

Tolan asked: "Anybody know who killed Guthrie?"

"No. But it won't matter. Houston will punish every settler in Corbin County for it."

There seemed no answer to that, so Tolan made none. He sat down at the table and began to eat. He was hungry, but somehow the food choked him this morning. Because it was Manette's food; because a traitor and spy had no business eating it.

He finished quickly. Going out, he said: "I'm riding to town this morning. Roan ought to be back before long, though."

Manette nodded, asking no questions about Roan's whereabouts. Tolan got his horse saddled and led it to the bunkhouse. He packed his personal things in his blanket roll and tied it on behind the saddle. Then he mounted and rode out toward town.

Well, this job was done, the spying part of it anyway. Maybe Roan was through with it altogether. But Tolan knew he wasn't. There would be another job ahead, a big paying gun job. And he'd be needing money. Since last night, he knew he'd be needing money. Because, riding back toward Manette's last night, he had made up his mind to one thing. Beth was not going back to singing in a saloon if he could help it. She was going to get her chance to break away.

She could sew, she said. All right. She'd have her chance to try earning her living that way. But she'd have to have new clothes first, respectable clothes, not the kind percentage girls wore. She'd need enough money to rent a shop and buy material. She'd need enough to live on for a while until her dressmaking started to pay. Tolan didn't know how much it would take. But he did know that he'd get it, however much it took.

Damn, this new experience of wanting to do something for someone else gave him a lift! But would Beth accept it from him? That was the catch. Riding steadily, he tried to dream up reasons why she should accept. One after another he rejected them as flimsy, unbelievable. And then he hit on the one that really had bottom to it. He'd ask her to marry him.

But afterward, doubt came creeping in. Hell, why should Beth marry him? He wasn't handsome, not by a hell of a sight. He didn't have a lot of money, and he wasn't even very young. Why should she even consider it? Well, maybe she wouldn't. But you didn't win a poker pot by folding your cards. She'd put in a rough night last night. First the thing at the Custer, afterward Hubner chasing her, and after that the gunfight in the empty house. *Maybe today's a good day to ask her,* Tolan thought. *Maybe even I might look good to her today.* She'd never shown him any particular affection. But she'd seemed to enjoy his company.

Encouraged, he nudged his horse into a trot. Suppose she did accept him? Well, he just wouldn't go through with it right away. Not until after the showdown that Houston was bound to have with the settlers. Tolan figured he might not even come out of that scrap. And he was damned if he'd make her a widow before she'd even had a chance to be a bride. Still, if she thought he was going to marry her, maybe she'd take the money he gave her and use it to set herself up in the dressmaking business. He'd tell her he was an awful gambler and put it to her like it'd be a favor to him.

Just outside Antelope Junction, he saw Roan Childress leaving town. He pulled up his horse and waited, his thin lips smiling at last.

Roan hurried after he spotted Tolan, and, when he got there, Tolan asked: "Well, how'd it go?"

Roan said: "I found out where the cattle went, if that's what you mean." He related the happenings of the night as briefly as possible. Before he had even finished describing his escape from Zulke's four riders, however, Tolan said: "How about Beth? You just came from town. You seen her?"

"She's all right. She's at Guthrie's."

"How the hell'd she get out there?" Tolan almost shouted, suspicion and jealousy flaring like tinder.

Roan thought—*Here we go again.*—and said carefully: "I headed in to Guthrie's Spur this morning after a fresh horse. I found Beth alongside the road wrapped up in a buffalo robe. She'd spent most of the night there."

Tolan studied Roan narrowly. "How the hell did she get there?"

"She was riding with Guthrie. When Guthrie got shot, the horse bolted. Beth was thrown out."

Tolan snarled: "You're lying, damn you. Beth wouldn't get in a buggy with Guthrie." He paused, breathing hoarsely, his mind feeding on an almost insane jealousy. "I've seen you lookin' at Beth. Damn you, Childress, what'd you try with her? What'd

153

you do to her?"

Roan said with weary patience: "Earl, take it easy. I tell you she's all right. Go on out to Guthrie's and talk to her if you don't believe me."

"I will," Tolan said. "I will. And you'd better be giving it to me straight. Because if you're not, I'm coming after you."

Roan said wearily: "Do what you damned please. You're a fool, Earl. You wouldn't believe anything bad about that girl in your home town, Ruth Gilroy. Now you won't believe anything good about Beth. You were wrong then, and you're wrong now. I hope Beth sends you packing. Because you'll make her more miserable than Hubner did." For a moment he thought Tolan was going to hit him. Deliberately he fished makings from his pocket and began to fashion a cigarette. When he had it lighted, he said: "Houston's got my list. I wasn't going to give it to him. I even gave him back his money. But Coates slugged me and they took it."

Tolan managed somehow to drag his thoughts away from Beth. He said, sour and unbending: "So now Houston's through with us. Damn!"

"Looks like it. I'm through with him, anyway."

"What are you going to do?"

"Stay on with Manette, if he'll let me after I tell him what I've done. Try and help out when the showdown comes. What about you?"

Tolan frowned, the dregs of jealousy still souring his attitude. He said: "Manette can't pay us over thirty a month. Houston will be paying gun wages. I'll take them."

"You want money that bad?" Roan could scarcely keep contempt out of his voice. "You'd live at Manette's all winter and then hire out to kill him?"

Tolan refused to meet Roan's eyes. He said defensively: "I gave my word to Houston. Remember?"

Roan snorted.

"And Houston gave me his word," Tolan said.

"You didn't hire out to murder settlers," Roan said. "You don't have to stick. So there must be another reason."

"So there must be another reason," Tolan mimicked savagely. "Damn you, Roan, why don't you keep your nose out of my business?"

Suddenly the night's weariness stole the last of Roan's dwindling patience. He snapped: "All right. I will. Hire your gun out if you want. Kill the men who've been your friends. I sure as hell hope you enjoy the money you get paid for doing it. Only don't get in my sights, because from now on you're just another of Houston's killers. Is that straight?"

"You're damned right it's straight. And let me tell you something. If you've laid a hand on Beth . . . well, I'll be at Manette's before dark lookin' for you."

Anger had built unreasonably in Roan, yet strain and fatigue stunted all other emotions. He seemed unable to feel regret over this open break with Tolan. He sat his horse, glaring coldly at the man who had been his friend, amazed that until now he had not been able to see this wholly selfish side of Tolan, this cruel, unfeeling attitude. He said: "Takes a man a long time to figure things out. Took me a long time to figure you out. But I've got the job done now. If I never see you again, it'll be too soon."

"Likewise."

As a pair of fighting cocks, they braced each other fiercely. Then Tolan whirled and rode off without speaking. His spurs sank cruelly into his horse's sides. In minutes he was only a speck, pounding across the plain in the direction of Guthrie's Spur Ranch, by-passing the town altogether.

Roan rode slowly toward Manette's, slumped a little in his saddle. His open sheepskin flapped in the gentle wind. Occasionally he passed over a muddy spot turned soft by today's warmer air and the thin sunlight, and his horse's hoofs slid beneath him. He didn't notice.

His mind kept searching for things he could do, things that might ease this intolerable situation. He asked himself—*Coates? How about Coates?*—and knew at once that it wouldn't help at all if he killed Coates. The death of one man meant little now. Nothing he could think of would have much effect now.

Troubled, aching and weary, he rode into Manette's yard. He heard Manette out at the barn, shoeing a horse. The steady ring of sledge on anvil was a pleasant, busy sound that relaxed his grim features.

He dismounted and hesitated, hating this, hating to face Manette and speak his piece. But at last, squaring his shoulders unconsciously, he went into the barn.

Manette looked up as he came in. "Where's Tolan?"

"Gone. He and I have been working for Houston. Tolan is still working for him." He said it all in a rush.

Manette smiled. He laid down his sledge and tongs and sat on a section of peeled log that was used for a chopping block. He said: "Most men do what they think is right. Sometimes they're wrong, but, hell, they're only men." His bearded face and finely chiseled features, his gentle eyes and his air of unhappy tolerance suddenly reminded Roan of something, something he could not quite place. A picture, maybe, remembered from long ago, from boyhood. "How about you?" Manette asked.

"I won't make excuses," Roan said. "But I want you to know how it was. Rustlers cleaned me out in Montana, cleaned out the herd that would have paid my mortgage installment in the spring. Houston came along about that time and the banker put him onto me. He wanted me to come in here and gather evidence against rustlers that he said were stealing him blind. I agreed, and he promised to pay me six hundred dollars for four months' work. He paid it in advance when I arrived in Antelope Junction." Roan paused, not looking at Manette. Then he said: "I gave him the six hundred back today. I meant to tear up the list I'd made, but Coates came in the door behind me and slugged me with his gun barrel."

"Why didn't you want to turn the list over to Houston? Isn't that what you were paid to do?"

Roan marveled that Manette could keep his tone so calm. He said: "Houston has no intention of prosecuting the men on that list."

Manette seemed to sag. His shoulders slumped and his face fell into lines that were slack and hopeless. It was a long time before he looked up at Roan. When he did, he said: "It will all be on my shoulders when it happens. I planned that raid."

Roan did not contradict him. "I'll get going," he said.

Manette stood up. "No. Don't go. Unless you feel you have to. If you'd like to stay on. . . ."

"I would. But how about the others?"

"They needn't know." He looked at Roan steadily. "You might not come out of this alive. You know that, don't you?"

Roan nodded.

"Then it's settled. Let's get busy and finish shoeing this horse. Lilac will have supper on pretty soon."

XIX

After leaving Roan, Tolan rode hard. He skirted the town and picked up the road on the far side of it.

He felt sorry now. He'd made an enemy of Roan and it was too late to change it. And he felt afraid, the closer he came to Guthrie's, afraid that Beth would turn him down. A cold knot formed where his stomach ought to be and his ribs seemed to squeeze the breath out of his lungs. He hadn't been this scared in years.

Many times, over the last two miles, he almost lost his nerve. Twice he halted. But each time he went on. He dismounted before the porch. Hat in hand, he mounted the steps and knocked on the door. He had to knock three times before the door opened.

He saw a woman, Mrs. Guthrie, he guessed, and said: "Ma'am, you got a girl here named Beth MacPherson?" He saw the suspicion in her eyes, and said hastily: "You ask her if she don't want to see me. Tell her it's Earl Tolan. I just got to see her, ma'am. I got to."

Pleading came hard to Tolan. He did it awkwardly. But Mrs. Guthrie could not fail to see his sincerity. She said: "Come in, Mister Tolan. I'll see if Beth is awake. She had a frightening night, so I'll have to ask you to be very gentle with her."

"Oh, I'll be that, ma'am. You see. . . ."

"Yes, I do see." Mrs. Guthrie smiled. "Now sit down and make yourself comfortable."

Tolan went in and sat down. Guthrie's two sons peered at him from a doorway, solemn and unblinking. Tolan felt hot and embarrassed. He was not used to surroundings such as these. Neither was he used to the company of good women and children.

Suddenly he recalled the way Beth had run away last night during his shoot-out with Saul Hubner. Suppose she refused to see him? What would he do then? He'd only been a boy when he had met Ruth Gilroy. In a boy's way, he'd loved Ruth. But lordy, what a difference there was between a boy's love and a man's!

Mrs. Guthrie came back. Beth wasn't with her. He jumped up, swallowing hard, but Mrs. Guthrie smiled at him.

"Beth will be along in a few minutes, Mister Tolan. She

wanted to freshen up a bit."

Tolan turned his hat around and around in his hands. Mrs. Guthrie called her two sons to her. "It's almost suppertime, boys, and I need wood for the stove. Don't you stop now until the wood box is full."

"*Aw,* Ma! We wanna. . . ."

She clapped her hands. "Move, you two!"

They shuffled out. Tolan looked at her gratefully.

She said—"I have things to do."—but studied him again before she left. In her eyes, Tolan saw doubt, and speculation, and perhaps a bit of worry.

He said: "I'll not hurt her, ma'am."

"Please don't. Singer or not, she's a lovely girl."

"I know." He didn't know what else to say, and so he just stood there silently, waiting. Mrs. Guthrie went away, and after a while the slightest of sounds made Tolan turn.

He saw Beth at the foot of the stairs, as timid and frightened as a doe. Tolan took a step forward, then halted abruptly. He said: "You all right, Beth?"

She nodded, wordless. Her large eyes regarded him unblinkingly, as if she were trying to read his thoughts.

He said: "I've been worried. I've been worried sick about you."

"Why?" Her voice was a whisper.

"Why? Well, hell. . . ." He shrugged helplessly. "I ain't much for talkin' to a woman, Beth. I can't make up fancy words. I only know what I feel. I . . . I like you, Beth. You like me at all?"

"Yes." Some of her fear appeared to be leaving her, and the slightest bit of color came into her face.

Tolan sighed. "Well, that's good. I didn't know." He hesitated over what he had to say next, then blurted—"I want to marry you, Beth. . . ."—and rushed on before she could reply: "Oh, I know I ain't much for a girl like you. But I'd take good care of

you, Beth. I'd never let nothin' or nobody hurt you. You can bet
your life on that." Beth opened her mouth to speak, and terror
struck at Tolan. He said: "Wait a minute, Beth. I got to tell you
the rest of it. Then you answer if you want. Or think it over a
few days." He paused for breath and, not looking at her, went
on: "There's going to be some trouble here in Corbin County
over that business last night. I'll be gone most of the time till
it's over. So maybe you'd wait. Maybe you could open a
dressmaking shop for yourself."

He looked at her, then. Tears stood out in her eyes. She was
shaking her head. She murmured: "I want to, but I'd only make
you miserable. You're jealous, and you haven't enough faith."
She smiled with an effort. "But I'm glad you asked me." For a
while silence hung between them. Then Beth said soberly: "You
need a woman. There can't be any doubt about it, not one like
me that's worked in saloons."

Tolan felt a knife edge of pain. Roan had told him substan-
tially the same thing. *Get yourself an ugly woman that no one else
wants*, Roan had said. *Then you can be sure.*

He said humbly: "I never doubted you, Beth. I doubted
myself. I couldn't see why a girl like you would even look twice
at a man like me, when there were so many better ones around.
But can't you see? If you'd say you'd marry me, then that
wouldn't bother me no more. I'd know different. You see?"

Beth gazed at him, a painful indecision in her eyes. Seeming
to decide something in her mind, she came across the room and
laid a hand on his arm. He could almost feel its warmth through
the heavy sheepskin. His heart thumped, fast and uneven.

Beth said timidly: "Ask me again, Earl."

"Sure. Marry me, Beth."

"You're sure you'll have no doubts?"

"About you? Not ever. Not me."

Suddenly she began to cry, and his arms went around her,

trying to quiet her trembling. She whispered: "Yes. Yes, I'll marry you, Earl."

Tolan guessed he'd never understand a woman. If it made her that sad, why had she said yes? He swallowed and patted her back. He said—"It's settled then."—trying to control the hurt that sickened his heart. "I got to ask a favor of you. Might be all winter before we can get married. You can't go back to the Custer an' you'll have to live. You start up that dress shop you want. I got a little money that I'd only lose gamblin'. You take that and use what you need of it to get yourself going. All right?"

She looked up, her eyes swimming. "Well," she said doubtfully, "I don't know."

He gripped her arms. "Look. You kind of belong to me now. You got to do what I say."

"All right, Earl."

There seemed nothing further to say. An awkward silence stretched out, until Tolan picked up his hat from the floor where he'd dropped it. "I'll be going. I'll see you when you feel better and get back into town. You send me word out at Colonel Houston's place."

"Good bye, Earl." She raised her lips for a kiss.

He kissed her. He went outside and closed the door behind him.

His horse had wandered halfway across the yard. He walked to the animal, picked up the reins, and mounted. He started to ride out, but Mrs. Guthrie called from the kitchen door: "Mister Tolan!"

He rode over, his face bleak with hurt because Beth had cried when she accepted him.

Mrs. Guthrie said: "You don't know much about women, do you, Mister Tolan?"

"I guess not, ma'am."

"You don't know that they cry sometimes because they're happy?"

"Do they?"

"Yes, they really do. She'll make you a fine wife. See that you make her as good a husband. Just because she sang in the Custer doesn't mean. . . ."

"I know," Tolan said, humble but sure of himself at last. "She'll never regret marryin' me, ma'am."

Tolan rode away then. For the first time in a good many years he had a powerful reason for wanting to live. For the first time in his life, he belonged to someone, and was needed. But Beth would need money to get herself started, and Tolan had given his word to stay with Houston until spring. Tolan never broke his given word.

XX

That same night, Colonel Simon Houston sat alone in the sitting room of his hotel suite and stared blankly at the wall. Occasionally his lips moved, and occasionally he scowled blackly. Coates came in about 10:00, tipsy with drink, and tried to talk with him. The colonel's answers were short and preoccupied, and finally Coates left and headed down the hall toward his own room.

The colonel didn't go to bed until after 2:00, but his plans were complete. Tomorrow, he would leave for Cheyenne.

He awoke at 5:00 a.m., as he always did. It was still dark outside, but he did not light a lamp. He moved quietly lest he wake his daughter in the next room. Dressed, he tiptoed out of his bedroom and into the small sitting room, carrying his boots in one hand, his gun and belt in the other. He sat down on the sofa and pulled on his boots. He stood up again and belted the gun around his middle.

His sheepskin and hat hung from a tree beside the door. He

took them down, then let himself out into the hall. Stopping at Coates's door, he turned the knob and pushed. The door was locked. He knocked, and heard the sibilant sounds Coates made inside the room as he came toward the door.

Then it opened and Coates stood in the doorway, a gun in his hand. Houston said with exaggerated irritability: "Put that damned thing away!" He shoved Coates aside and went into the room.

Dawn was a faint gray pall in the room now. Houston could see the tall gunman, his hair rumpled with sleeping, his eyes fuzzy. Coates yawned. "What the hell's the matter?" he asked, and scratched the matted hair on his chest through a hole in his red flannel underwear.

Houston said: "I'm going to Cheyenne this morning. I've got a lot to do, so I may not be back for a while. I want you to take Janet home, and then I want you to stay there. No trouble and no gun play, do you understand?"

Coates shrugged, and yawned again.

"When you hear from me," Houston said, "I want you to get Sykes, Riordan, Jones, Harrison, Peters, and McKinley and come to Cheyenne."

He had named the deadliest of the men employed by the large ranchers in Corbin County.

Coates's yawning mouth closed with a *snap* of teeth. "What's up?"

"You'll find out. Just stay out of trouble and come when I send for you."

He went back to the door. He thought of the stranger, Childress, with a touch of baffled anger. He said: "Stay out of trouble unless you get a sure thing on that Childress."

Coates grinned. "That'll be a pleasure."

Downstairs, the clerk sipped at a cup of black coffee and looked sleepily over its rim at the colonel. The dining room exuded sharp odors of frying sausage and coffee. Houston went in and sat down. He ordered sausage and flapjacks, and ate wolfishly when they came.

Afterward, he went out into the cold gray dawn. He walked to the livery stable, chose a big, leggy bay gelding from the string of four that he kept here, and had the animal saddled. Minutes later he cantered out of town on the south road, the one that led to Casper, where he would catch the train.

Two days after his arrival in Cheyenne, Houston addressed a group of prosperous-looking men in a paneled back room of the Cheyenne Club. Their names, called off, would have sounded like a reading from the who's who of Wyoming Cattlemen's Association. The air was rich with the smoky aroma of fine cigars, with the elusive fragrance of Scotch whiskey and tooled boot leather.

Houston waited, pompous and solemn, until the murmur of talk subsided. "I've called you all together tonight," he said, "because the situation in Corbin County has become intolerable. Jerome Guthrie, bringing home a load of Christmas gifts for his children, was shot in cold blood because he happened to bump into a bunch of rustlers stealing his cattle. That same night there were six separate raids on different ranches, all of them dummies to cover a bigger steal of five hundred of Guthrie's and five hundred of mine." He paused for breath and glared at his sobered audience. "As you no doubt know, a few weeks before that, Otto Zulke, a man caught red-handed rustling from the Five Star outfit, was acquitted by a court in Antelope Junction. It has come to this, gentlemen. Either we fight or we tuck our tails between our legs and crawl out of Corbin County. You can take your pick, of course, but, by all that's holy, I'm going to fight!"

A murmur of approval rose in the room. A man called: "Fine!

But how are you going to fight rustlers when you don't even know who they are?"

Houston smiled triumphantly. "Gentlemen, I do know who they are. I know the name of every man who participated in those raids the other night. I hired a couple of range detectives and one of them made a list."

A serious voice asked: "What do you plan to do?"

Houston said: "There is only one way left to us. We'll form a force of fighting men and sweep through Corbin County. Those of the rustlers who will, can pack up and leave. Those who will not leave, who resist us, must die. We will burn every squatter shack in the county."

There was another murmur, a shocked one, of mixed approval and disapproval. But Houston gave them no opportunity for discussion. He said: "Upon my arrival here in Cheyenne two days ago, I sent telegrams to every fighting man I could think of within a reasonable distance from here. Already some of them are arriving. When they are all gathered, they will be augmented by men from your own ranches in Corbin County. We have friends in the state government here, gentlemen, and need fear no reprisal from the law. Only in Corbin County is there danger for us, that danger lying in the control these rustlers have over the county government. But when the rustlers are gone, when we have done our job, then the county government will no longer dare to move against us."

He sat down. Another man took the floor and made an impassioned plea to the group to go along with the colonel's plan. Then another to whom the colonel had previously talked.

A dissenting voice was shouted down.

The colonel got up again, and harangued them on the vital necessity of the step he wished to take. The attractiveness of direct action, of violence that appeals to all men began to work its dark magic. Murder had been committed and had gone unavenged. Every man in the room had lost cattle to the settlers. And gradually, mob fever infected the entire group. The brutal cold-bloodedness of the plan was overlooked in the excitement. And Houston left the room with a promise of support from every man in it.

Houston's recruitment of his force prior to broaching the subject here had purpose in it—purpose he did not disclose. His Army experience had taught him that men often will agree to violence in the quiet of a conference room only to renege when the violence becomes reality. Houston's plan called for a force already in being, to whom violence was commonplace, and who would not quail at its reality. Houston would command the expedition and he proposed to make retreat impossible once it started.

Excitement made him feel younger than he had for some fifteen years. He found himself remembering other expeditions during his Army days. A campaign was a campaign and he intended to enjoy this one.

XXI

After so much excitement over such a short period of days, things seemed ominously quiet in Antelope Junction. Weeks was buried in an icy plot in the town's cemetery, and no one went to visit his grave. Guthrie was interred in the burial plot at Spur along with a baby girl who had died in infancy and a cowpuncher who had been killed in a fall from a horse. Guthrie's grave was visited often by a grieving and saddened widow.

Beth MacPherson returned to town. She rented a small two-room house and prepared to take in dressmaking work, which came in not at all from townspeople reluctant to forget that she had sung in a saloon.

A week of quiet, just long enough for the settlers to grow complacent, to begin the planning of another large raid on the

Association members' stock. But now, it was not Manette who led them, but rather a cocky, confident Russ Conover, made reckless by the undetected murder of Guthrie.

At Pitchfork, Colonel Houston's ranch, Coates grew nervous and irritable. Janet, sobered and saddened, grieved in spite of herself over the way she had sent Childress from her, and avoided Coates. Recollection of the colonel's orders hobbled Coates for almost the whole week. But his nervous nature and his natural dislike of enforced idleness were now aggravated by anticipation of the action that the colonel's plan promised.

Coates oiled his gun, saddled up, and rode toward town. He was looking for trouble and he meant to have it. It was a rather warm day for mid-winter in Wyoming. Underfoot the snow thawed, turning the road to mud.

Coates pressed his horse hard, and mud flung up in huge gobs from the animal's hoofs. In the speed of the horse, and the smell of the air, Coates found an intoxication stronger and headier than that of liquor. He hoped Childress would be in town, but when he stepped into the Custer, he saw only three men belonging to the settler faction. Otto Zulke, Ernie Cassel, and the Mexican, Ramon Jiminez. Well, they'd do.

Coates stepped up to the bar and ordered a drink. Everett Dowd slid him a bottle and glass.

Cassel and Jiminez watched him fearfully, but Zulke scowled at his drink. Speaking to no one in particular, Jiminez said: "It's too warm. Storm coming."

Everett Dowd nodded profoundly and mopped the bar with a rag. Ransom Coates laughed. Cassel and Jiminez looked away. Coates said: "Everett, you're not very damned particular who you let drink at your bar."

Zulke whirled, leaving his drink, and headed swiftly and wordlessly for the door. Jiminez muttered a soft excuse in Spanish, and followed. Cassel would have followed too, but Coates's hand came out and caught him by the collar of his sheepskin.

"I just stopped by for one drink," Cassel babbled. "I got to get home."

Coates laughed. "You got some butchering to finish, I reckon?"

"No, no, honest, Coates, I never stole a single head of cattle." Panic fluttered in Cassel's deep-set eyes.

Coates flung the man to the floor. He said: "Cassel, you're a dirty, thieving, son-of-a-bitch. You haven't got the guts of a jack rabbit. But you killed Guthrie, and now I'm going to kill you."

He didn't really think Cassel would draw, and not even Coates was foolish enough to kill a man who didn't. But the meanness in the depths of his brain had to come out some way. He wanted to watch Cassel crawl.

Cassel lay on the floor like a dog on its back, cringing and waiting to be kicked. He unbuckled his gun belt and rolled away from it.

Most men would have been sickened, but not Coates. Cassel's display of utter cowardice only fed his cruelty. He moved toward Cassel and sank his boot toe in Cassel's belly. Cassel groaned and hugged himself against the pain. Coates kicked again.

Behind the bar, Everett Dowd said in a tight, scared voice: "Coates, quit it. Please quit it."

Coates put his pale gaze on the bartender. "You going to make me, Everett?"

Dowd's pride fought a battle with the instinct of self-preservation. Pride lost. Dowd turned away, ashamed.

Cassel did not take advantage of the distraction, or even try to get away. He just lay like a well-whipped dog, waiting, waiting for the punishment he knew he must take to stay alive. Coates turned back to him and deliberately kicked him in the groin. Cassel's scream sounded muffled and choked off. He doubled up.

Coates said: "You're the one that killed Guthrie, ain't you, Cassel?"

"No! It wasn't me. I swear. . . ."

"Then who was it?"

"I don't know. I don't know. I wasn't there."

"Cassel, you're a liar." Hard, but not too hard, Coates kicked him in the face. "Who was it?" He was enjoying this, simply as an outlet for his festering meanness. But suddenly the thought struck him: *I'm on to something. Cassel really knows!*

Cassel covered his face with his hands and began to blubber. Coates made a scuffing noise with his feet, and Cassel's hands came away from his face and lay idle, waiting to protect himself from Coates's next kick. Coates brought the heel of his boot down on Cassel's wrist.

Cassel screamed louder this time, very near the breaking point. He yelled frantically: "All right! All right! I'll tell you. It was Russ Conover. I was with him and I saw him. It was Russ Conover. Now will you let me go?"

Behind Coates, Dowd's voice, unexpectedly firm, said: "Yeah, Coates. Let him go. I've got a Greener pointed right at your belly and I'd sure like to squeeze off the trigger."

Coates froze. His lips barely moved. "All right, Cassel. Get up and go home. Don't do any talking or I'll get you when I've finished with Conover."

"Sure. Sure. I won't say a damned word!" Cassel crawled halfway to the door on his hands and knees. He shot a glance at Coates over his shoulder, got up, and ran the rest of the way.

Short seconds later, Coates heard his horse pound away from the saloon. Everett Dowd said: "Coates, this Greener is going to be on the bar top from now on. If you put your head inside that door. . . ." He left the threat unfinished.

Coates turned and stared at him, stared until he saw Dowd

begin to break, despite the shotgun in his hands. Then with a short laugh, he whirled and made for the door.

Conover, he thought. *Well, I'll be damned.*

He considered riding out to Conover's right away. But the day was young and he still had a week-old thirst to tend to. Chuckling, he headed for the hotel bar.

Everett Dowd waited until the door closed behind Coates. Then he laid aside the shotgun and hurried to the door. A padlock hung from a chain, and he slipped it into the hasp, and snapped it shut. With that done, he picked up the shotgun and headed for the back door.

Maybe Conover had killed Guthrie. Dowd didn't know. Right now he didn't care. He just hated Ransom Coates and wanted to thwart him. He locked the back door with another padlock and hasp, and then slogged down the alley toward the livery barn, keeping a weather eye out for Coates's tall form.

He rode out of town on his short-legged black mare, taking the south road that led past Manette's and on to Conover's spread. Dowd, a law-abiding man, would not have warned Conover against the sheriff. But this was different. This was a lot different.

XXII

The quiet week had not lulled Sheriff Gustav Orr into any false sense of security. Rather, it sharpened his sense of impending disaster. Five days ago, he had wired Fort McBurney begging for immediate help. Two days afterward he had received a reply, stating that no men were available for martial law duty in Corbin County, and also that, after reviewing the facts as outlined by Sheriff Orr, the seriousness of the situation did not appear to warrant military intervention. However, the telegram stated, in view of Sheriff Orr's apparent concern, a Captain Wilhite was being detached from the fort and would arrive in Antelope

Junction shortly to review Orr's facts first-hand. Later, but only if the captain so recommended, troops might be detached from the fort and dispatched to Corbin County. The telegram had brought a fatalistic shrug from the sheriff, and a deepening sense of depression.

Colonel Houston had been gone a week. Probably by now he had the Association members firmly united behind him. Quite likely he had gathered a fighting force and was ready to act. Furthermore, Ransom Coates had not been in evidence in Antelope Junction since the colonel's departure. To Orr, this meant that the colonel had left orders for him to stay out of trouble, to hold himself in readiness for whatever action the colonel planned. Also, as if conditions were not already bad enough, the settlers were getting cocky, and from the furtive way their conversations stopped whenever he approached, Orr suspected they were planning something. No matter how he tried, he could not stop worrying.

Naturally a wave of relief washed over him when, on the same day Coates chose for his trip to town, a uniformed cavalry captain dismounted in front of the courthouse, peeled off his gloves, and came up the steps. Orr saw him from the window of his office, and met him at the door.

"Captain Wilhite?" he asked before the captain had a chance to speak.

The captain nodded. Orr said: "I'm Gustav Orr, sheriff of Corbin County. And, brother, am I glad to see you!" The captain's eyebrows raised faintly at that, but then he grinned. He came into the sheriff's office, and shrugged out of his heavy greatcoat. He said: "Now, what's this all about, Sheriff? I don't mind telling you, I've had a damned hard trip."

The sheriff offered him a cigar, which he took and lighted after carefully biting off the end. He was a tall man, this captain of cavalry, and he had an air of quiet confidence about him. Orr felt better already. He marshaled his thoughts and began at the beginning. He told of Zulke's acquittal, of Weeks's and Guthrie's murders. He told of Childress's success in obtaining the names of the men participating in the big raid, and of Houston's threat regarding it.

After he finished, the captain stared at him thoughtfully for a long time. The captain's eyes were brown and intelligent, but they could be very hard. He said: "Sheriff, you have told me nothing to make me believe that martial law is justified. The things that have happened are things properly within your own jurisdiction."

Orr tried to be patient. "Captain, you don't know Colonel Houston. He's coming back, and, when he comes, he'll bring a small army with him. I can't stop an army, Captain. I can't stop them and I damned well know it. I've got to have help."

The captain flexed his wide shoulders. He spread his hands expressively. "But with no more evidence than you have, Sheriff. . . ."

Orr cried: "Man, do you have to see the streets of Antelope Junction running in blood before you'll believe me? Do you have to see bodies piled in a wagon? I know what I'm talking about. I know Colonel Houston and I know Ransom Coates. I know all of these big cattle raisers in this county. It's going to break, I tell you, and damned soon."

The captain grimaced skeptically. But he at last conceded: "Well, I am in no particular hurry to make that return trip to the fort. And my horse needs a few days' rest. Tell you what. I'll put up at the hotel and wait a while. I'll wait a few days and see what happens. But I warn you, if nothing happens and I find no proof that something will within two weeks, I'll have to go back."

Orr started to argue, but he saw it was no use. He mustered a smile. "All right, Captain. I guess that's fair enough."

"Good man. Now I'm going to find a bed and sleep around

172

the clock." The captain shook Orr's hand and went out. Orr saw him mount his horse and ride toward the hotel.

Discouraged, he sank into his swivel chair and stared bleakly at the wall. His prospects of receiving help from the Army seemed dismal indeed. Even if this Captain Wilhite did finally get around to seeing evidence of trouble with his own two eyes, it might be too late to send to the fort for troops.

At last Orr got up, convinced that he had done all he could. The hand had been dealt. Now it was time to pick it up and see what kind of cards he held.

With deep preoccupation, he locked his office door and went out into the street. He walked over to Main, paused, and lighted a cigar while he idly surveyed the street's length. Nothing caught his attention, so he continued on down Main.

As he passed the telegraph office, a man with a green eye-shade inside gave him the high sign. He went in.

The operator waved a yellow scrap of paper at him. "Sheriff, is Coates in town?"

"Haven't seen him," Orr said.

"If you do, tell him there's a wire here for him, will you?"

"Sure." Orr started to go, but didn't. "Who's it from, Abe?"

"Colonel Houston."

"*Hmmm.* What's in it, Abe? If it's important, maybe I'll ride out that way and give it to him."

Abe pushed the eyeshade up on his forehead. "We ain't s'posed to give that out. But, hell, you're the law, an' I guess it'll be all right. It says . . . 'Meet me in Cheyenne at once.' " Abe smiled. "That's all there is to it. You reckon it's important, Sheriff?"

Orr shook his head slowly. "No, I don't guess it is. Well, if I see Coates, I'll tell him. 'Bye, Abe."

He went outside, knowing that Houston was ready and would

begin to move. The thing had begun, and he could not do a single thing about it.

Roan Childress was working on a gate that crossed Manette's lane when Russ Conover pounded up to it at a steady run. Roan swung the gate wide so he could go through. He caught one glimpse of Conover's sweaty, wild face, then thumbed back his hat and stared after him as he thundered in toward Manette's cabin. Concern touched him. He picked up his tools and slogged afoot toward the house.

He came into the yard, left his tools in the barn, and kept on going. He could hear shouting inside the house, and hesitated. Maybe Manette and Conover wouldn't want him butting into a private discussion.

Then the door opened, and both Manette and Conover came out. Conover yelled: "Damn it, Philo, I tell you he's after me! Everett Dowd rode out just to tell me that. Coates got to kicking Ernie Cassel around the Custer this afternoon and Ernie spilled his guts."

Manette's voice held an enforced calm: "Did you kill Guthrie?"

"Yes! Yes! Sure, I killed him. What would you have done that night if a guy'd come out of nowhere and started blasting away at you? You'd have shot back, wouldn't you?"

Manette seemed tired. "Yes . . . I guess I would."

Conover made a frantic, confused gesture. "What am I going to do, Philo? I can't stay here. Coates will kill me. I've got to hide, or get out of the country. And I've got to do it damned fast."

Manette said: "All right, Russ. Go on out to the corral and saddle up two horses. Catch that big bay mare for a pack animal. I'll have Lilac get some things ready."

"T-two horses?" Conover stammered.

"Yes. I'm going with you. I'll see that you get clear, Russ, because it's mostly my fault you're in this jam."

Childress stepped up. "How about me, Philo? I could go with him."

Manette shook his head. "A mistake was made. I made it. I owe Russ my help."

His tone told Roan his decision was final. He gave up and moved away to help Conover with the horses. Manette went into the house.

Lilac stood at the stove, stirring something in a pan, but Manette knew she could not have told him what she was stirring, or why. She said in a dull voice: "You're going with him."

"Yes. I'll need. . . ."

"I know what you'll need, Philo. Get the horses. I'll have it ready."

"Yes." He hesitated, his hand on the doorknob. He knew his leaving was hurting Lilac. She was afraid, not for herself, but for him. She knew Coates, knew also that whoever was with Conover when Coates caught up with him would receive no more mercy than Conover did. There would be no escape for Conover or anyone who fled with him. Not in winter, when tracking a man was so ridiculously simple a child could do it. Not when there was not even the slightest prospect of a storm to hide their tracks. Lilac knew all of that.

Manette left the door and crossed the room to her. He said gently: "You wouldn't have me send him off alone, Lilac. You wouldn't have me desert him. Guthrie fired at him first, and, while that doesn't excuse murder, Conover wouldn't have been anywhere near Guthrie's if it hadn't been for me. A man has to accept responsibility for the things he does, Lilac. That's all I'm trying to do."

She turned, soft and womanly, with her heart's pain plainly in her eyes. She fought a losing fight against her overwhelming desire to plead with him, and said: "Philo, please. I can't let you go."

"You can't stop me."

"No. I suppose I can't."

A coldness began growing up between them. Manette said: "Lilac, don't let me go this way." He touched her shoulder. She whirled, burying her face against his broad chest, sobbing. She tightened her arms about him and pressed her body almost frantically against his, as though by this she could hold him, keep him. But he remained unyielding, and at last her shoulders sagged and her arms relaxed. She raised a tear-wet face and murmured: "All right, Philo." She managed a small smile and brushed at her eyes. "I'll be good now. Get the horses ready and then come in for your provisions."

Manette felt a vast pride in her, mixed with shame for himself. He growled—"Behave yourself while I'm gone."—and stomped over to the door.

Outside, Roan had two horses saddled, good animals, the best in the corral. He had a big bay mare in the barn as Manette walked up, and was cinching down a pack saddle.

Conover kept walking out of the barn and looking up the road. He was so nervous he couldn't stand still. He kept saying: "Hurry up. Hurry up, damn it. Let's get out of here."

Manette got the canvas panniers down from their nails on the barn wall and lugged them to the house. Roan led the pack horse up to the door, and after a few minutes Manette came out with the panniers filled and hung them on the pack saddle. Roan lashed them down.

Conover mounted one of the horses and took the lead rope of the pack horse from Roan. Manette said: "Ride out if you want, Russ. Head south. I'll catch up in a minute." Conover moved away, and Manette turned to Roan. "See that she stays safe, will you?"

"Sure. You know where you're going?"

"South toward Casper, I suppose. We'll spend some time trying to hide our tracks and probably hole up in some line camp cabin and wait for a storm."

Lilac came to the door, her eyes dry, her face very pale. Manette walked over and took her in his arms and kissed her. Roan turned away.

Then Manette mounted and ran his horse out of the yard, not looking back. Roan watched him ride over a rise of land. He heard Lilac Manette crying softly as she went back into the house. Roan cursed savagely, under his breath.

XXIII

Roan stayed and ate supper at Manette's, but after he finished, he rose from his chair and said: "Missus Manette, you'll be all right here by yourself. But I've got to lend a hand in this. If it'll make you easier in your mind, I'll be glad to take you to town, or maybe to some neighbor's where you can stay until I get back."

She shook her head. "What are you going to do?"

"I don't know yet. I'll have to plan as I go along." He picked up his hat and went out into the night.

He had not been completely truthful with Lilac. He did have a plan of sorts. First, he intended to go into Antelope Junction and ask Orr to deputize him. After that, Coates—arrest Coates on an assault warrant and throw him in jail. Next, find Manette and Conover, and arrest Conover for the murder of Jerome Guthrie. Conover was, after all, the one who had pulled the trigger. It would not help Conover if Manette died with him at the hand of Ransom Coates. Above all else, Roan wanted to save Philo Manette's life, and this was the only way he could see to do it. He had to do it, or die trying. He couldn't live with himself any more, idle and haunted by guilt.

He caught his horse, saddled and bridled, and set out at a brisk pace for town. As he rode, the moon poked up over the eastern horizon, cold and yellow and almost full. And at 9:00 p.m., he came into the main street of Antelope Junction.

He found the sheriff in the Custer Saloon, along with half a dozen townsmen. Playing stud poker for nickels and dimes, Orr looked bored by the game and worried, too. Roan walked over to him and said: "Can I see you a minute, Sheriff?"

Orr got up, stretched, and yawned. "Deal me out, boys. Another time." He followed Roan outside. "What's on your mind?"

Roan said: "Sheriff, you probably know this. Coates worked on Cassel today and Cassel accused Conover of killing Guthrie. So Coates is after him. And Manette's with Conover."

"So?"

"I don't want Manette hurt. Pin a star on me, Sheriff, and I'll bring you Coates on an assault warrant. Then I'll go get Conover for you."

The sheriff gave a dry laugh. "Just like that, huh?"

Roan looked at him steadily. "Have you got a better idea?"

"Coates will kill you."

"Maybe. Maybe not. You going to give me that star? Or do I go on my own?"

Orr cracked his knuckles and shifted his weight from one foot to the other and back again. "All right," he said finally. "Come on over to the office."

As they walked, Orr talked. "Coates was in town today, all right. But I didn't know about Ernie Cassel until a couple of hours ago. After Coates beat up Ernie, and Ernie blabbed, Everett Dowd closed up the Custer and rode out to warn Conover. I didn't hear about the beating until Dowd got back, and by then Coates was gone."

They reached the courthouse and the sheriff unlocked the

door. He lighted the lamp on his desk and began rummaging in the desk drawers. He said: "Coates got a wire from Houston telling him to come to Cheyenne. Don't know if he's gone yet or not. Maybe you can still catch him."

Roan asked: "Have you seen Tolan today?"

Orr nodded, grinning faintly. "Today and every day. If he didn't leave with Coates, you'll find him over at Beth Mac-Pherson's new shop."

Roan hoped Tolan would stay clear of it when he went to Houston's after Coates. He intended to ask Tolan to do just that.

Orr found a tarnished star and handed it to Roan, who pinned it on. "Raise your right hand," Orr said in a bored voice. "Do you solemnly swear to uphold the law to the best of your ability, so help you God?"

Roan nodded.

Orr said testily: "You're supposed to say . . . 'I do.' "

"I do, then."

Orr grunted: "All right, go on." But he added as Roan went out the door: "Good luck to you."

"Thanks."

Roan hurried over to Main, turned off on a side street, and strode on to the small house before which hung the sign: *Dressmaking. Beth MacPherson.* He didn't see a horse tied to the hitching post before it, so he knew Tolan had left. Trying not to let worry dig into him, Roan went back to the hotel and wheeled his horse away from the hitch rail.

The horse jumped with fright at the touch of the spurs and raced out of town. Taking the road to Pitchfork, Roan fretted because already he might be too late. A wire from Houston calling Coates to Cheyenne might mean nothing at all. But if Tolan went along, too, then it almost certainly meant that trouble was about to begin. He might be too late to stop that trouble. He could only try.

He held the horse to a steady gallop, careless of the slippery footing beneath the pounding hoofs. By moonlight, the road before him showed the hard-pressed prints of both Tolan's and Coates's horses.

Riding into Pitchfork's big yard, he was quite aware of the chance he took. Pitchfork's crew would side Coates in any showdown, and the best he could expect from Tolan was neutrality. He rode directly to the bunkhouse and swung down from his horse.

The bunkhouse door opened and a man peered out, calling: "Coates? You back? Forget something?"

Roan said: "No. I'm looking for Coates. Has he left for Cheyenne already?"

"Yeah. Over an hour ago." The man came out, short, bowlegged, wearing a week's growth of graying whiskers. He was chewing tobacco and he spat on the ground as he peered at the visitor. When his eyes became accustomed to the outer darkness, he said: "Hey! Ain't you the feller that kicked hell outta Ranse?"

"We had a fuss," Roan admitted.

"An' you're lookin' fer him now? Man, you oughta be glad he's gone."

"Maybe I should. Miss Janet up at the house?"

"Yeah." The man spat again and went back into the bunkhouse.

Walking toward the big house, Roan figured that Coates must have taken all of Pitchfork's hardcases, leaving behind only the ordinary cowhands.

He saw a lamp burning in the kitchen, so he went to the back door and knocked. Janet opened the door. "Mister Childress! What are you doing away out here?"

"Call me Roan," he said. "It sounds friendlier. Or are you still . . . ?"

"No, I'm not angry with you any more. It seems that you were right." She stepped back from the door. "Won't you come in?"

She wore a full-skirted gown of cotton gingham, red-and-white-checked. She looked fresh and clean, but she also looked very tired.

Roan walked right into a rich odor of chocolate cake. He grinned. "Isn't it kind of late to be baking?"

"Yes. But it makes me forget my worries. I don't know why you're here, but I presume you know that Ranse and Earl Tolan left here about an hour ago with six of the worst characters in Corbin County."

"Who were they?"

"McKinley, Harrison, Peters, Jones, Sykes, and Riordan. Ranse had the crew out all afternoon rounding them up." She opened the oven door and peered in at her cake. Straightening, she presented the perfect picture of a disillusioned and unhappy girl. She murmured: "I didn't think he was capable of it. Oh, Roan, I've lived with him all my life and loved him, and I thought I knew him. But he means to ride through Corbin County exterminating settlers the way you would rats. It's horrible. It's too horrible to believe. And yet I have to believe it." She shuddered.

Roan took her arms in his hands and pulled her close to him. "Try crying," he said. "Stop holding it in. I've got a shoulder for you to cry on."

She smiled up at him shakily. "I'll cry later, Roan. Right now, we've got to think of some way to stop it."

"I thought I had a way tonight. But I got here too late. There's only one way left."

"And what is that?"

"I'll go to Casper. When they come, they'll come by train to Casper, and ride north from there. I'll wait until they arrive. I'll see what direction they're taking. Then I'll ride ahead of them and warn the settlers who live along their route of march. I'll gather the settlers together and at least put them on their guard. That way, it won't be a slaughter anyhow."

"Roan, that's terrible. It will be just like two armies."

He nodded. "No help for it now."

Like fire, their need seized them then. It grew hotter with the contact of their lips. Roan said: "Janet, whatever happens, I'll be back." He drew away abruptly, knowing that, if he did not go now, he would never go. He tried to smile, and failed. He realized that his fists were clenched.

Janet's voice was a mere whisper: "I'll be waiting, Roan."

That promise lingered in his mind all the rest of that night. He rode steadily southward, sometimes drowsing loosely in the saddle, sometimes wide-awake. Yet always she seemed close to him, the softness of her body under his hands, the eagerness of her lips, so warm and womanly and well-remembered.

Dawn came, and cold, cheerless sunup, and still he rode steadily on.

In mid-morning, angling across a long, low hill to cut out a bend in the road, he crossed the tracks of three horses, two of them obviously ridden, the other led. Conover and Manette, he thought, and followed the plainly marked trail. They, above all others, needed to be warned of Houston's impending advance.

This rolling sagebrush country was quite different from the land around Antelope Junction: Bands of antelope dotted the plain, and cattle were almost as numerous. Occasionally Roan spotted a cluster of ranch buildings in the distance, a wagon toiling along on the road, or a herd of wild horses, heads high and tails whipping in the wind. But always before him, the three-horse trail went on.

Noon came, and hunger pangs twisted at Roan's stomach. At last he sighted a tiny, log line camp cabin ahead, and guessed that Manette and Conover would have stopped here. He rode openly until he came within rifle range. He drew no fire, so he went on.

A light, vaporous plume of smoke rose from the cabin's rusted tin chimney.

Roan hailed the cabin without dismounting: "Hello, the cabin! Conover! Manette! Is that you?"

He was nervous and uneasy, for he knew how quickly hunted men get on their triggers. He sat his horse, quite still for what seemed an eternity. Then he rode close and dismounted, still edgy. He kneed open the door and stepped inside.

The place had a musty, moldy smell. The floor was of packed earth, the roof of sod. He saw a couple of rusty bedsprings on the floor at one end, a rickety table in the room's center. On one wall hung a weather-grayed cupboard with a front that swung down and hung on chains to form another, smaller table.

A sheet-iron stove, rusted through, sat in one corner. Roan put his hand on the stove and felt heat. There was a skillet on the stove, partly filled with beans that were still warm. And in the oven he found a pan containing two burnt biscuits.

Roan took out his pocket knife and began to eat. He finished the beans, scraping the pan clean. He choked down both biscuits. Then he went back out and stared around.

Seeing nothing significant, he mounted his horse and began to circle the cabin. Behind it, he found a spring. He dismounted, knelt, and took a long drink. Remounted again, he continued his circle. Then he picked up the tracks of the three horses, heading westward.

He sighed with relief. He had thought, at first, that Conover and Manette were holed up in this cabin, which lay directly along Houston's probable line of march. But if they had gone on, headed west, then all was well.

Roan continued southward, and at dusk came into Casper, lying on the bank of the North Platte River and at the foot of the Haystack Mountains.

He checked the railroad station first, verifying the fact that today's Cheyenne-bound train had carried Coates and Tolan and six other Pitchfork men. He got the schedules of trains arriving from Cheyenne for the next week, then registered at a small hotel, went to bed, and promptly fell asleep.

XXIV

In the cold, gray, first light of dawn almost a week later, a train pulled into Casper, whistled mournfully, and ground to a screeching halt.

The town slept, but not Roan Childress. For days he had haunted the train yards, watching each newly arrived train from Cheyenne. And today, his ceaseless watching paid dividends. He saw Colonel Houston climb stiffly down from one of the coaches, cocky as a bantam rooster, to stand, spraddle-legged, while he watched the crew he had collected walk back to the boxcars and begin to unload horses.

Roan did not need to recognize the men of this crew. He did not need to know their names. They bore a stamp, all of them, a wild and ragged look that plainly shouted: hardcase, border cut-throat, gunman. Each man carried a rifle. Each wore a low-slung revolver. Each had his own peculiar economical way of moving.

This then was how Houston had spent the past two weeks. He must have scoured most of Wyoming and Colorado to gather a crew such as this. It could not have been easy, nor could it have been cheap.

Roan felt cold, watching. Fifty horses were jumped down from the open boxcar doors. Fifty saddles slapped their backs.

Fifty men stepped into leather and rode the cold weather antics out of their mounts.

Up through the northern bluffs they went, out onto the rolling, sagebrush plain, riding into the teeth of a sudden storm.

For Roan, it was watch, and trail, and circle now, for he needed to know just what route Houston's party would take. He hadn't guessed wrong regarding Houston's intentions, yet the thought gave him little satisfaction. From the look of Houston's crew, they figured to travel fast by the most direct route, but he couldn't afford to guess.

At a mile-eating pace, and with grim purpose, the column filed northward. Snow slashed against them, driven by a very stiff wind from the north. At times their shapes blurred and almost disappeared in the driving snow. Roan watched, and rode into their trail, and followed.

He followed all that morning, staying back far enough to avoid discovery by stragglers. Houston's party nooned a few miles short of the line camp cabin where Roan had found the beans and biscuits more than a week ago.

Now, Roan believed, he had an adequate idea as to the party's direction. They were headed for Philo Manette's place, by an arrow-straight route. And it stood to reason that Manette would be Houston's first intended victim.

He left the trail then, circling around the party for the hard ride to Manette's. His first duty was to clear Manette's wife out of the cabin, and take her into Antelope Junction, where she would be safe. After that, he must alert the settlers, gather a force of them, and get ready to engage Houston's gunmen.

Circling, Roan forgot that Houston had learned his military tactics while fighting plains Indians. He overlooked the standard Army practice of throwing out scouts to ride wide on both flanks of a column.

Head down in the driving, stinging snow, he did not see them until he rode into the middle of them. He heard a hoarse shout: "Hey, you! What the hell you doin' 'way out here?"

Roan glanced right, then left, discovering one man about ten feet away on his right, another a little farther to his left. Caught unaware, just as Roan had been, both men were frantically clawing aside their heavy coats, trying to get at their guns. Roan sank spurs into his horse's sides and headed directly between them.

Their guns cleared as he reached a point midway between the two. They held their fire momentarily for fear of hitting each other, but as Roan drew away, presenting his broad back as a target, they raised their cocked weapons and fired, almost as one. Surprise, the driving snow, and too much haste put their aim off just a little. One bullet missed cleanly. The other entered the neck of Roan's horse.

The horse bogged his head as his front legs collapsed under him. Roan pitched forward and landed, rolling in the snow. The horse catapulted, end over end, and a flailing hind hoof caught Roan a glancing blow on the side of the head.

His head slammed down into the ground. He tasted icy mud and snow, and that was all.

Dimly, as consciousness returned, he heard Houston's bull bellow rolling across the camp: "All right! Ride! We've wasted enough time!"

He was on a horse, thrown across the saddle like a sack of grain. They were bringing him into the camp.

He heard Houston's irritable voice again, nearby this time. "What the hell's this?"

"Snooper, Colonel. But we nailed him."

"Is he dead?"

"Naw. Fall stunned him is all."

Roan heard another voice, the even, deadly voice of Ransom

Coates, and knew by the man's tone that Coates had recognized him. Coates said: "Dump him off that horse." Roan heard the sound of a gun cocking.

One of the flankers lifted Roan's feet and dumped him unceremoniously off the horse onto the ground. The horse side-stepped nervously away. Roan looked up, saw Coates raise his gun, sighting, and knew that, if he moved now, he was dead. Houston called: "Wait! Who the hell is it?"

Coates's voice was venomous—"It's that son-of-a-bitch Childress."—and drew his careful bead.

Roan's muscles tightened involuntarily against the smash of the bullet. Everything in him shouted for action. He tensed, ready to make a convulsive movement that might throw him out of the path of Coates's bullet if he timed it right. He slumped again as a horse pounded up and slid to a stop between him and Coates. The horse reared, his hoofs coming straight down at Coates. Coates dived out of his saddle to avoid them, landing on hands and knees in the snow. And then Roan saw Tolan.

Tolan looked at Roan briefly, coldly, then yelled at Coates: "Hold it!" Tolan held his gun, steady and cocked, in his hand. It was trained, not on Coates, but on Houston. He said: "Tell that trigger-happy fool to get back at the tail end of the column, Colonel. You can bring Roan along, tied if you want, to keep him from getting away and spreading the word. But you'll not kill him. You'll not shoot him down while I'm alive."

Getting up, Coates snarled: "That won't be long, bucko."

"Maybe," Tolan said. "Maybe not. Tell him to move, Colonel."

Houston's voice was tight and rebellious. "If I don't?"

"Why, I'll kill you, Colonel. It's that simple. Tell him!"

There was a silence. Then Houston said: "Go on, Coates."

Coates shuffled away. Houston glared at Tolan. "You'll pay for this," he said, and wheeled away.

Tolan shrugged and returned his gun to his holster. He

dismounted, walked over to Roan, and looked down at him, saying nothing. A man started to pass him, leading a horse. He said—"Find yourself a spare, mister."—and grabbed the reins from the man's hand.

The man started to protest, but Tolan's chill eyes changed his mind. Tolan looked down at Roan again. There was no sympathy in Tolan's face, no softness, no trace of lingering friendship. "Get up," he said.

Roan struggled to his feet.

"Slug me and take my gun," Tolan said. "Don't bungle it or they'll tear me to bits."

Roan stared with surprise and dumb lack of comprehension.

"Damn you," Tolan snarled. "Don't stand there gawking. Do it!"

Wordlessly Roan drove his fist into Tolan's throat. He followed it with another, before Tolan could fall, another that landed flushly on Tolan's jaw. As Tolan fell, his eyes glazed.

Roan stooped, snatched Tolan's gun from its holster. Dizzy from the exertion, he straightened and vaulted into the saddle of the nervous horse Tolan had commandeered for him.

He heard a yell: "Hey! He's runnin' for it! Kill him! Kill that . . . !"

He wheeled the horse and sank spurs into the startled animal's sides. A bullet cut through the loose folds of his sheepskin, but he scarcely noticed it. He lay low on the horse's withers, concentrated on zigzagging the horse as it fled for the obscurity of the driving snow curtain and thin timber to the side of the column.

A bullet burned his shoulder and another drilled cleanly through one of the horse's ears. Then he was clear, and riding harder than he had ridden ever before in his life.

His spurs drew streams of bright blood from the horse's sides. The horse flattened out and ran with every ounce of power he possessed. Every time the horse showed signs of slowing, Roan would rake him again. And when that failed to keep the animal at top speed, Roan would belabor his rump with the quirt that he had found hanging from the saddle horn.

He rode with total disregard for the hazards of the plain, jumping the horse over arroyos and dry washes where a slip or miscalculation would have meant death or disablement for both man and horse. He disregarded the treacherous ground underfoot and deviated not at all for thickets of cedar and jack pine that loomed in his path. His very recklessness was all that saved him, for some among his pursuers would not risk the washes that Roan jumped and they lost vital time in circling and hunting for a safe crossing. The result was that they lost his trail in the driving snow before he had covered even the few miles that separated the invaders from the lonely line camp cabin. They spent valuable time trying to pick it up again, and, when they finally found it, Roan was a mile ahead of them, within sight of the cabin.

But looking down at it, Roan felt suddenly sick with despair. For a plume of smoke spiraled from its chimney, and the bay mare Roan remembered so well was tied to a tree beside the cabin. He had planned so carefully. Conover and Manette should have been a hundred miles from this tiny cabin now. He should have been running well ahead of the deadly column, carrying the news of its approach to the settlers of Corbin County. And yet here he was, with a scant mile of grace, trying to decide whether or not he could risk a stop at the cabin to warn Manette and Conover.

There was really no leeway for decision. He flung a wary glance over his shoulder and saw the vanguard of his pursuers. They had sighted him, had abandoned the trail and were now galloping directly toward him.

He spurred the tiring horse toward the cabin, ahead of him

and somewhat to his left. A bullet *buzzed* like a bee twenty feet to his right, and shortly thereafter the report reached his ears, flat and wicked in the cold thin air. *Damn it, why did the snow have to thin just now? Why couldn't it have stayed thick and blinding for just a few minutes more?*

A quarter mile to the cabin. And what would he find there? Conover and Manette with their boots off, their horses unsaddled in the corral, too many things to be done before the pursuit surrounded the cabin and covered it with their rifles?

Someone came to the door of the cabin and disappeared. Then both men came to the door.

Roan could not repress a snort of disgust. Manette and Conover *did* have their boots off. Neither wore his gun. Riding in, Roan raised a shout: "Get your horses! Houston's less'n a mile away!"

They darted back into the cabin. It seemed an eternity before they reappeared, running, belting guns around their waists as they ran. Roan reached the cabin and flung himself from his horse. Manette was tugging a saddle from a lean-to at the side of the cabin. A rifle bullet *thudded* into the log wall.

Roan flung a quick look behind him. Hell, they were less than a quarter mile away. This must be another bunch from the column, riders who had separated from the others and ridden ahead, paralleling his course without knowing it. The rifle shots must have fetched them and now they were on hand to bag three men instead of one.

He said quietly: "Forget the saddle. We'll never make it now."

"You go on," Manette said. "Maybe you can. . . ."

Roan pointed. Even as they stood watching, the bunch split, half of them coming on, the other half riding full tilt to head off possible escape. Roan said: "In the cabin, quick. We can at least hold them off a while."

Conover dived inside. Manette nodded at Roan, grinning

wryly. "Go ahead."

Roan walked deliberately into the cabin. Manette followed without haste, closed the door, and dropped the bar into place.

For a long five minutes, no shots came. Peering cautiously from the cabin's single window, Roan saw the attackers spread out, surrounding the cabin.

Roan tried to estimate how long it would take for Houston to bring up the main body. He guessed half an hour. If the whole force stayed to see the siege through, there was at least a bare chance of someone escaping in time to spread the alarm. If the bulk of the column went on, there would be no chance at all.

The minutes ticked away and at last a new fusillade of shots broke the silence. Bullets tore into the cabin walls. Instinctively all three men flung themselves to the floor.

"Throw down your guns and come out!"

Manette laughed and rose to the level of the window sill. He bellowed: "You'll have to come and get us, boys!" He ducked.

Another shower of bullets buffeted the cabin. Conover began to gasp loudly for air. "Easy," Roan said. "You wouldn't get ten steps from the door if you went out there."

He levered himself up, flung a quick shot from the window, and dropped to the floor again, grinning. Fate had presented him with a beautiful target the instant before he fired—Houston standing, spraddle-legged, at the edge of the scattered timber a hundred yards away. He hadn't hit the colonel. That would have been too much to expect. But his bullet had kicked up snow and mud at the colonel's feet, and the colonel had taken an undignified dive into the nearest clump of brush.

Now the affair was personal. Houston would stay and see the siege out, and that might save the settlers. But Roan's grin faded. This spelled almost certain death for Philo Manette, Russ Conover, and Roan Childress.

★ ★ ★ ★ ★

Riding into sight of the cabin, Tolan took in the scene warily. At Houston's order, the force dismounted orderly, quietly, efficiently. Horses went to the rear, out of range, to be picketed and rested for use after the cabin's occupants had been slaughtered.

Without seeming to, Tolan kept glancing to right and left, even as he prepared to add the fire of his own rifle to those of the others. He was looking for Coates. He knew Coates would be looking for him.

He saw Coates. He got lazily to his feet, even though he might be hit by a bullet from the cabin. Standing tall, he waited until Coates saw him.

Coates rode up to him and dismounted. He was covered with mud, and so was his horse. That meant a spill, which would not have improved Coates's temper. Tolan grinned tightly. He knew what was coming, knew Coates's reputation, yet he felt no fear. He trusted his own gun speed. The old excitement, the old challenge stirred him. Here was a man supposed to have a draw like light. But was he really as fast as they all said? Tolan wondered.

Beth had no place in his mind now. This was the core of living. This was the seed of intoxication. Steady, he waited, and he grinned mockingly when Coates said: "That was a put-up job. You let him slug you and take your gun. You knew I'd kill him first chance I got."

"Yeah," Tolan said. "First chance you got to back-shoot him. Or the first time you found him with his hands tied."

There was purpose behind this baiting of Coates, coldly calculated purpose. Make your opponent mad, if you can, because then his anger will hasten his hand, blur his judgment, ruin his aim. Tolan said softly: "Coates, there's a streak down your back as yellow as your eyes."

He saw Coates's eyes narrow, this being a flicker of the eyelids and nothing more.

Tolan's hand streaked for his holster, but his mind streaked also, functioning with lightning speed. Even before his hand reached the holster he knew it would be empty. He had allowed Roan to take his gun. Grogginess from Roan's blows must have made him forget. . . . Motion was beautiful and continuous in Tolan. Even before his hand encountered the empty holster he was flinging himself aside, his head swiveling, his eyes searching the ground from which he had just risen. He fell, but it was more a dive than a fall. His right hand closed on the rifle receiver even as Coates's first bullet took him in the back. His body smashed against the ground, pinning the rifle down. He went numb, but he put forth a torturing effort and rolled, seeking to bring the rifle to bear. He didn't quite make it. Something like a gigantic fist slammed him in the chest just under the heart. And eternal blackness came down like a curtain over his eyes.

XXV

During one week in which she had been in business, Beth Mac-Pherson had welcomed exactly one customer, a woman who asked her to pin a straight hem in the bottom of a new gown. She had charged the woman nothing. And every day she put up a brave front before Tolan, assuring him she was swamped with work.

But after Tolan left for Cheyenne, tears seeped into her eyes in spite of herself. She knew why customers didn't come in. She was a dance-hall girl. No matter how hard she tried, she would never bridge the gap between herself and the respectable ladies of the community. She could almost hear their whispered comments as they passed her shop: "Involved with that awful man, Hubner . . . killed because of her . . . can't tell me that where there's that much smoke there ain't some fire." She stood it for another week—the sitting, the staring out the window into the bleak street, the idleness, the thinking. And suddenly she could stand it no more.

Had there been any hope at all, she would have stayed. But there was no hope. In almost two weeks she had earned not a single cent. *I'll go to Cheyenne,* she thought. *They don't know me in Cheyenne, so maybe I'll be able to make it there.*

It took her most of the night to get ready. She packed her dress goods and her own clothes in boxes. Early in the morning she had them taken to the stage depot for shipment on the first stage to Casper. Then, dressing herself warmly and carrying only a small carpetbag, she walked to the livery stable and hired a horse.

She would ride to Casper and take the train from there. Had she announced her destination, the liveryman would have tried to stop her, for he knew better than she what a grueling long ride it was. But Beth's pride insisted that she slip out of town with as little notice as possible, and, besides, she could feel the tears burning just behind her eyes and knew they would burst forth upon the slightest provocation. The liveryman helped her mount, giving her a very personal stare, and she rode away, taking the long road south. The gray day, cold and raw and cheerless, did nothing to improve her spirits. She wondered if Tolan were still in Cheyenne, and if she would see him there.

Not ten miles out of Antelope Junction she began to wish she had waited for the stage. Not used to riding more than a mile or two at a time, she suddenly found the saddle exceedingly hard and bony, and herself exceedingly tender. But she would not go back.

Noon came and passed. Once she got down, knelt clumsily beside a stream, and drank from her cupped hands. She remounted with such difficulty that she determined not to get down again.

At 5:00, nearly exhausted and still a considerable distance from Casper, she heard the faint, flat echo of a shot. It came from off to her right, and at first she paid it little attention. But when she heard a dozen more in the space of half a dozen breaths, she halted her horse and nervously stared in the direction from which they had come. She remembered snatches of the talk she had heard, the uneasy talk that had been buzzing around Antelope Junction for a week. She recalled Tolan's vague mention of trouble and his too-warm farewell when he left for Cheyenne. Even Beth knew that no one shoots a dozen times at an antelope. In fact, a dozen shots indicated at least two guns, probably more. Yes, a fight was going on, a shooting fight between two groups of men. It took no particular astuteness to guess that Colonel Houston's men, including Earl Tolan, had engaged a force of settlers.

Beth knew she could not ride on, then. Earl was in danger. Maybe if a woman rode up, they would stop fighting for fear she would be hurt. She turned off the road in the deepening gray of fading daylight, and rode toward the sounds of shooting.

She rode for twenty minutes, guided by the firing, and with her agitation and fright steadily increasing. At last, reining up in a thick clump of brush, she could look down upon the lonely cabin and the men surrounding it. The size of the force that surrounded the cabin astonished Beth. Even from where she sat she could count over twenty men, and that must not be all of them.

She felt an immediate sympathy for the men in the cabin, even though Earl must be on the other side. And she knew with a cold touch of fear that when the occupants of the cabin had been killed or captured, Colonel Houston's men would move on to other lonely cabins. Breathless, she eased her horse back through the brush and spurred away. The weary horse's willingness to run puzzled her, until she realized that he knew he was at last heading homeward.

Then began the nightmare of tortured muscles, of weary, heavy-lidded eyes, of pain and torment. Beth had been in the saddle for almost ten hours already, and she still had many hours to go. Yet if she did not carry a warning back to Antelope Junction, the settlers would be trapped in their little cabins, trapped like those poor men in the one behind her.

Dark came, and Beth let the horse have his head, trusting him to find the most direct way to Antelope Junction. She did not even care when he left the road. She dozed in the saddle, and awoke, and dozed again.

At midnight, she came into Manette's yard. She had no idea at all where she was, but seeing the light in the window she could not resist its beckoning welcome, its promise of a few moments' rest.

Her horse nickered shrilly, and the door opened, throwing its square of light upon the ground. Mrs. Manette came running to her and helped her down from the saddle. Beth would have fallen, but for Lilac's strong supporting arms. "Where in the world have you been, child? What are you doing out alone at this hour of the night?"

Beth sagged as she reached the kitchen. She sank into a chair and pushed her hair wearily away from her forehead. Her voice was hoarse from disuse. "I was going to Casper. I was almost there when I heard shots. I rode toward them. There must have been fifty men . . . shooting at a little cabin. I came back to warn. . . ."

But Lilac Manette had stopped listening. She ran into the bedroom and came out again, shrugging into a heavy sheepskin. She cried breathlessly: "Stew and biscuits in the warming oven. Then you go to bed." She tied a scarf over her head, and then she paused just long enough to pat Beth's hand. "I know what they've been doing to you and your dressmaking shop. But that's going to change. When all of them know they owe their lives to you, I think you'll find things quite different."

Before Beth could reply, she was gone.

Lilac Manette ran across the yard with a frantic urgency. By the time she caught a horse from the corral, she was almost in tears. Even now she might be too late. With fumbling, clumsy fingers she unsaddled the horse Beth had ridden in here and transferred saddle and bridle to her own animal. Then, mounting astride without regard for her long gown, she pounded out of the yard and headed for Zulke's.

It took almost an hour of hard riding. She began screaming for help as soon as she came within earshot of the cabin, and just screaming made her feel better.

A light flickered inside the house. Zulke came to the door clad in long, red-flannel underwear and carrying a rifle. Apparently unconscious of his attire, as Lilac was, he listened to her brief, almost hysterical story.

"You reckon it's Philo an' Russ, ma'am?"

"Who else could it be, away down there?"

He turned back then into the house. Lilac could hear him giving crisp orders to his three half-grown sons. "Karl, Sam, Fritz, get out and saddle up, quick. Ride fast and see as many of our neighbors as you can. Get each of them to ride out on their own and gather more. I want all the men I can get here at dawn. Tell them Houston's on his way with fifty gunmen and he'll kill everyone he finds in his path."

Since Lilac refused to stay at Zulke's, he directed her to two nearby ranches and went himself to two others. The chain of warning had been set in motion. By morning, there would be enough settlers here to fight the colonel's column. But would

morning be soon enough to save the men besieged at the lonely
line camp cabin?

The morning after Roan rode out toward Casper, Janet Houston
ordered the buggy hitched up and drove away toward Antelope
Junction. She could not seem to stand living in this house where
her father's presence was so very tangible even in his absence.
He had destroyed all her respect.

She was asleep in her hotel bedroom when Lilac Manette
rode into town. She did not awaken at once, but as the confusion and turmoil grew in the streets, she stirred and opened her
eyes and listened. Her heart sank, for the street noises told her
as plainly as words that the townspeople and settlers were going
out to meet her father's approaching force.

Suddenly she had to know how the warning of her father's
advance had arrived in Antelope Junction. Had Roan brought
it? She prayed that he had, but some uneasy prescience told her
he had not. Quickly she dressed and combed her hair. She
slipped on her heavy coat and went downstairs. Mrs. Manette
sat on a heavy, leather-covered sofa in the lobby, and before her
stood Sheriff Orr, a cavalry captain, and a milling crowd of
townspeople.

Janet hurried to Lilac Manette. "How did you get the news?"
she asked breathlessly.

"Beth MacPherson brought it."

Janet felt the blood leave her face. "Is there news of Roan? Or
of your husband?"

Lilac shook her head mutely. Then Janet heard Orr speaking
to the cavalry captain. "You see, Captain Wilhite? I was right.
And now it's too late for you to help."

"Not necessarily," Janet broke in. "You are all the law that's
left in Corbin County. And the captain here represents the
authority of the United States Army. Between you, you may be

able to stop it."

"Two men?" Orr snorted. "Miss Houston, you're out of your mind."

She asked coldly: "Do you have a better plan?"

Wilhite spoke for the first time. "What makes you think we can stop it, Miss Houston?"

She smiled, without humor. "My father spent many years in the Army. He respects few things, but the Army is one of them. Convince him that, if he persists in the course he has chosen, the Army will hunt him and his men down, and you may be able to stop him."

"And who will stop the settlers?" Orr asked.

"You will. You are the settlers' sheriff."

Orr looked at Captain Wilhite. Wilhite grinned faintly at Janet. He said: "Miss Houston, we'll try. Come morning, we'll sure try."

Janet turned to Lilac. "There are two bedrooms upstairs. Come up with me and try to get some rest."

She walked up the stairs with Lilac Manette and waited until Lilac had lain down, fully clothed, on one of the beds. Then she tiptoed to the door and went out into the hall. She did not intend to wait here in town for news. She intended to tag along behind Wilhite and the sheriff and do her own small part in halting the carnage. Her father respected the Army, but he loved Janet. Between her and Wilhite, they might be able to stop him. Unless he had gone too far already.

XXVI

Throughout the afternoon the siege of the cabin continued, with sniping and an occasional frustrated volley coming from the colonel's men. Earlier, Roan had knocked chinking from between the log walls on the three sides opposite the window, so now they were able to command a view on all four sides and keep the attackers at a respectful distance. Roan knew, however, that as soon as darkness fell, the impasse would end, for then the colonel's men would be able to approach and set fire to the cabin. When that happened, they would be finished.

Conover turned from the chink where he had stationed himself, and mumbled: "Maybe help'll get here before dark."

Manette laughed. Roan said: "Better forget that, Russ. Even if one of us had ridden to Antelope Junction before they caught us, help couldn't get here before noon tomorrow. By noon tomorrow this cabin will be a heap of smoking rubble."

Wildness grew in Conover's eyes. As he turned back to his chink in the wall, Manette glanced at Roan and shook his head.

It took something like this to bring out what was in a man, Roan thought. Manette knew he was going to die, but he rose above fear. Indeed, he showed considerably more humor and zest than he usually did. Conover, on the other hand, died a little with each passing moment. His last hours would be a torment of terror, and he probably would break altogether before the end. Roan felt a stir of pity for him.

Conover seemed to be firing to relieve his nerves, and Manette said curtly: "Russ, quit wasting ammunition."

Conover whirled. He held his rifle level in his hands. He screeched: "Well, what are you goin' to do . . . stay here like a pair of rats in a trap and wait for them to smoke you out?"

"Got a better idea, Russ?"

"Damn' right. You're damn' right I have. I'm goin' out."

Manette took a step toward him, but Conover menaced him with the rifle. Manette looked at Roan, and his eyes carried some message that Roan failed to understand.

Conover crossed the cabin, still ready with the rifle. He backed to the door and fumbled behind him for the bar. Manette took another step toward him.

Roan said: "Let him alone, Philo. He'll shoot."

Conover laughed raggedly. "Damn' right I'll shoot. So stay put, you two."

He got up the bar and flung the door open behind him. With a final bloodshot glare at Childress and Manette, he whirled and stepped outside.

Immediately he flung the rifle from him and raised his hands. He took half a dozen steps away from the door and yelled: "Hey! I give up! Don't shoot!"

Dangerous though the situation was, Roan could not help but recognize the grim humor of that. Still a boy, he thought, playing a boy's game. All through the afternoon Conover had labored mightily to convince himself that he was going to get out of this alive. Now he honestly believed Houston's men would hold their fire. This was Conover's bid for life, in the twilight of his boyhood.

Roan started toward the door, then stopped as rifle fire *cracked* savagely along the perimeter of the attackers' line. Conover twitched as the first slug struck him. He half turned toward the cabin, and Roan saw an expression of utter bewilderment, of complete disbelief. A second bullet tore into Conover's leg, and he stumbled and went to one knee. Still there was no pain, no twisting of his features, but only that petulant, child-like surprise. The third slug entered Conover's back and flung him forward upon his face.

Roan reached the door an instant after Manette plunged outside. A bullet slammed into the jamb beside him and showered him with stinging splinters. Manette swiveled his head around, saw Roan, and shouted: "Back! Cover me!"

Swearing bitterly, Roan rested his rifle against the jamb and fired as fast as he could work the loading lever. He did not lack for targets, and had the satisfaction of seeing one man fall, of hearing another's high yell of pain.

Manette stooped and gathered Conover into his arms. Then,

staggering under Conover's weight, he shambled toward the door.

Apparently Roan's accurate fire distracted the attackers just enough, for their bullets miraculously failed to hit Manette.

Manette stumbled as he lunged inside, falling across Conover's body. Roan slammed the door and dropped the bar. Half a dozen bullets tore through the wood, filling the cabin with flying splinters. One of these bullets *thumped* into Conover's body and brought a sharp intake of breath to his lips.

"He's riddled," Manette panted. "Riddled!"

"Yeah. Four at least. Get him on the table and let's see how bad they are."

Roan felt no hope for Conover's life, but they had to do what they could. Conover lost consciousness before they lifted him to the table. Roan peeled off his shirt, tearing it free.

"Forget it," Manette said. "A minute or two, and he'll be gone."

Roan stood still, watching the bellows of Conover's lungs weaken and slowly die. When they finally ceased to struggle, he said: "They didn't have to do that."

Manette just grunted. Roan picked up his rifle and went to the window. Until now he had shot to wound, to instill fear and respect for the guns in the cabin. Now he would shoot to kill.

Then he saw something on the horizon. "Manette! Come here!"

Manette leaped to the window.

"Over there at the top of that rise," Roan said. "In that clump of brush. Do you see what I see?"

"A woman? What's she doing out here?"

As they watched, the woman turned her horse and disappeared into the thick screen of brush behind her.

Manette said with obvious relief: "So the settlers will be warned. Now, my friend, all we got to worry about is our own skins . . . and keeping Houston here until that woman has time to get clear."

"Yeah," Roan said. He started firing again. "Wonder who she was?" he said, but the question was lost in a wave of return fire.

Quickly, thereafter, light faded from the sky and a cold dusk settled down over the bleak landscape. Roan's mind prowled, seeking solution much as a pacing, caged panther seeks a way out of his cage. How could they escape from the cabin before the flames drove them from it? Or, better still, how could they prevent Houston's men from getting close enough to fire it?

He said: "Philo, soon as it's dark, I'm going out. There's only one way of keeping them from firing the cabin. That's to be outside where we can stop them."

"Maybe we could get through them."

"Uhn-uh. They'll be expecting that. What they won't be expecting is what we'll do. The worst that can happen to us is that we'll stop a bullet, but we'll do that anyway before morning."

Manette grinned cheerfully. "It'll be a long night, bucko. But I'm with you."

Again Roan felt the tug of his strong liking for Manette. Morning might see them both dead. But at least they would have had the satisfaction of pinning Houston down here most of the night. If they just held him long enough for the settlers to be warned, death would not deny them all rewards.

XXVII

As soon as full dark fell, Roan and Manette crept outside. Within the hour they had a brief flurry with half a dozen men who came carrying dry brush and wood they intended to pile against the cabin walls. They sent the attackers back, carrying one of their number, a second limping along supported by two of his companions.

Next, Houston sent in a troop of mounted men, who raked the yard with a deadly, withering fire intended to cut the defenders down by its very intensity. Roan and Manette thwarted this simply by slipping into the cabin and waiting until the circling troop rode off again.

Houston seemed very sure, after that. His men came in carelessly, their arms loaded with more wood and brush. It was a little sickening to Roan, this cold firing into panicked ranks. But he thought of Conover, and did what had to be done. He let them carry their wounded away, and then two hours of quiet passed. Houston was figuring out his next move.

At last, a withering volley came from the attackers, and again Roan and Manette went inside the cabin. But this time the volleys dwindled quickly into desultory sniping. It seemed so inconclusive that it didn't make sense.

Roan spoke wonderingly into the darkness. "What the hell's he up to now? You think he's given up and gone on with his main force?"

For a moment Manette was silent. Then he said: "Could be. Or maybe he's working on another idea. At any rate, we're safe as long as he keeps throwing bullets into the cabin. He's not going to send men into that hail of lead."

"Unless the rifle men are aiming high, while some others are crawling in on their bellies."

Manette considered that and rejected it. "Too dark for accurate overhead fire," he said. "No, it's something else."

Minutes dragged into hours, and the hours labored on. In Roan, the tension increased intolerably. He could stand to fight. He could even stand to die if he must. But he couldn't stand this waiting much longer.

Still he waited, occasionally firing at a rifle flash, and at last the eastern horizon began to turn a deep gray. He was hungry, and thirsty, and inordinately tired. He hadn't slept for more than twenty hours, every hour filled with action and nerve strain.

Gradually the sky lightened, and the sun poked up over the horizon. Still they watched; still they waited. And nothing happened.

At last, near mid-morning, they saw the reason for Houston's delay lumber over the rise in the distance—two wagons loaded with hay and dry wood. This explained the night of comparative quiet. This gave promise of death to come.

The wagons would be unhitched, drawn as close to the cabin as was practicable, and set afire. Pushed and guided by men hidden behind them, they'd be crashed into the cabin walls. After that, it would be but a matter of time until the cabin became untenable. And then Roan and Manette would go out into the storm of bullets that had claimed Conover.

"Any ideas?" Roan asked.

"Nope. This time they've got us."

"You think that woman really went for help?"

"Who knows?" Manette shrugged wearily. He had reached a point, as Roan had, where almost any end would be welcome.

Now the fire from outside dwindled, and Roan and Manette watched the preparations for firing the cabin. Since the wagons had stopped outside effective rifle range, they did not waste ammunition shooting at them.

The horses were unhitched, and the tongues reversed so that they ran under the wagons instead of projecting in front of them. With this done, several men got behind each wagon and started them for the cabin.

It was eerie the way they came on, apparently self-propelled. Due to the slight elevation of the ground as it sloped in toward the cabin, the wagons completely concealed the bodies and legs of the men behind them. Roan and Manette had nothing whatever to shoot at. Only by some fantastic stroke of luck could their bullets go through two thicknesses of wood and hit the men behind the tailboards.

Roan did not even bother to shoot. Manette took a couple of shots, and then gave it up.

Manette shivered involuntarily, and Roan grinned at him. "Cold? You'll be warm enough pretty soon."

Manette returned his grin. "How long you reckon it'll take?"

Roan studied the walls of the tiny log cabin.

"I saw a cabin burned once in Montana to smoke out a killer. It was log, like this one, but the logs were some greener. It took about an hour and a half before the man came out. I'd say we had an hour."

The wagons came closer. Roan said: "The roof's sod. At least it won't catch and fall in on us. Worst we'll have to put up with will be the heat and the smoke. But a man can stand a lot of both when the only alternative is bullets."

Something bumped the near wall. Seconds later another wagon bumped the far wall. Roan and Manette heard low voices, and then the *crackle* of flames in loose hay.

Roan looked at Manette, a question in his eyes.

"No," Manette said. "I don't want to shoot them. It'd be murder and it wouldn't help us any."

So they only watched as the men scooted from behind the wagons and zigzagged frantically across the clear ground. Just outside rifle range, one of the fugitives stopped. Hands on hips, he surveyed the cabin, his very stance proclaiming his puzzlement. Then he turned and went on.

"We're a pair of damned fools," Roan growled. "They won't give us any breaks."

"Those few might."

Now, suddenly, with so little time left, the minutes began to race by. Little wisps of smoke drifted into the cabin and the temperature rose almost imperceptibly.

Twenty minutes passed, and suddenly Roan coughed. His

eyes began to water, and he began to sweat. An hour? Would they have an hour? He said: "We'd better get down on the floor. The air'll be better there."

He lay down on the cool earthen floor. Manette followed suit, and they breathed the purer air gratefully. Looking up, Roan could see the distinct dividing line between the pure air and the pall of smoke about four feet above the ground.

The fire crackled fiercely against the two longer walls. A tongue of flame came through a crack between the logs and licked against the inside wall.

Outside an ominous silence reigned—no shouting voices and no shots. Houston was sure of his quarry, just waiting for Roan and Manette to stumble out of the cabin.

Roan realized suddenly that the sun no longer shone through the cabin window. It had climbed to its zenith. He said: "It must be past noon. What's for dinner?"

"Barbecued settler," Manette said, and began to cough.

Roan guessed that almost an hour had passed since the cabin had been fired. He was beginning to feel light-headed. He knew time was short and, oddly, he felt almost glad. Going out would mean an end to imprisonment, an end to waiting. He had long ago given up hope of life.

The heat became almost intolerable. Both men were soaked with sweat, gasping shallowly for air, and drawing in only smoke and fumes.

Roan gathered his muscles under him. "Well, Philo?" Manette grimaced. "Now or never, I guess. I'm so damned dizzy, though, I'll probably fall when I get up."

Roan began to rise. He felt his holster for Tolan's gun and closed his hand on its grips.

As though in anticipation of their coming, shooting broke loose outside. Roan heard a confused, continuous shouting, and then the thunder of galloping hoofs. He said: "What the hell?

Can't they wait?"

Manette's scorched face twisted in an expression that Roan did not at once understand. Then he thought of the woman they had seen last night, and comprehended the hope that burned in Manette.

He crawled to the door, reached up, and raised the bar. He pushed the door ajar. What he saw brought him to his feet, made him fling the door wide, and step outside. The sudden wealth of fresh air nearly took his consciousness. He staggered and fell against the cabin wall.

Down the light rise from the north galloped a horde of settlers, shouting, shooting, riding with reckless abandon. Roan could see Zulke, and Cassel, and the Jiminez brothers, and half a score of others he recognized in the vanguard. They sent up a howl as Houston's invaders broke from cover and ran for their horses, scattering like a covey of startled quail.

But a core of Houston's hardest, his toughest, remained to cover the retreat, and these poured a deadly hail of fire into the ranks of the hard-riding settlers. A horse went down, flinging his rider a full twenty feet. A man raised in his stirrups, dropped his rifle, and fell kicking from his horse. Startled, they pulled up and, motionless, made an even better target for the hidden riflemen. Two more went down.

Roan began to run toward them, and now he became the target for the snipers. Bullets kicked up dirt at his feet, and *buzzed* past his head. He yelled: "Back! Take cover! Some of you circle to cut off their retreat!"

He reached them, untouched by the bullets that sought his body, and grabbed the reins of one of the riderless horses. They were dismounting, a few of them, and bellying down behind the clumps of low brush that dotted the landscape. Manette, who had followed Roan, took his place with these.

Roan vaulted to the saddle of the horse he had grabbed, rose in the stirrups, and waved his fisted revolver. For twenty-four hours he had stagnated in the tiny cabin, wanting action, and now all at once he was free. He yelled—"Come on!"—and spurred the horse off to the right, paralleling the line of snipers who were all that remained of Houston's force.

Reaching the end of that line, he reined left and rounded the end of their line, with fifty settlers galloping behind him. Ahead, the fleeing gunmen were spreading, scattering. He turned, standing in his stirrups, and bellowed: "I want ten men! The rest of you go after them. Bring 'em in alive, if you can, dead if you can't!" A dozen men hung back and rode to him. They reined up and waited for him to speak. He said: "We'll go in behind this bunch that's hidden in the brush. I don't think they'll hold out long."

But he had underestimated Houston's stubbornness as well as the size of the bunch that had taken cover in the brush. Now from the intensity of fire that *crackled* ahead, he guessed that at least half of Houston's men had remained behind—and they were picked men.

Roan's own men dropped to the ground, seeking what cover was available, and he became bleakly aware that his miscalculation could have disastrous effects. Had he let the escaping gunmen go, the fight would have come to a quick and decisive end. Now, it might degenerate into a costly, deadly war of attrition. Well, the mistake had been his. It was up to him to correct it.

For a moment he paused, a clear target atop his horse while he observed the terrain. He looked across the valley and saw three more riders galloping toward the cabin, looking toy-like in the distance. One he identified instantly as a woman. The second, blue-clad, might be wearing an Army uniform. The third? He guessed it was Sheriff Orr.

There would be an attempt, then, to halt the battle. Roan wheeled his horse to ride again around Houston's dug-in line.

209

What the four of them could do, he didn't know. He only knew they had to try.

He rode hard, an occasional bullet zipping within a yard of him. He rounded the end of Houston's line and headed toward the three oncoming riders. He heard the meaty *smack* of the bullet striking his horse and let his body go, loose and relaxed, in anticipation of the fall. The horse's head went down just as Roan kicked his feet from the stirrups. He sailed through the air with the solid *thump* of the horse's body in his ears, and then he was sliding on the muddy, snowy ground. A bullet showered him with mud, and he didn't stop his roll until he got a low clump of brush between Houston's guns and himself.

Roan eased his head and shoulders to one side of the brush clump, searching for the rifleman who had killed his horse with such a clean neck shot. He saw him, not twenty yards away, and tried to draw back. Smoke billowed out from the man's rifle muzzle. Roan felt a solid blow on his right shoulder, a blow that made him jerk away spasmodically. He rolled behind the brush clump, and put a hand beneath his coat. It came away sticky with blood.

But he had seen the man before he fired. He could not mistake those yellow eyes. Ransom Coates had shot him. Pain began to stab through Roan's shoulder. To one side of the brush behind which he lay, he saw a shallow gully. It seemed hardly deep enough to hide a man, but he slipped into it. He crawled ahead carefully, expecting the burn of Coates's bullets in his back, but knowing that, if he raised his head to locate Coates, he would be finished.

His only chance lay in changing his location. He needed a chance to stand, to shoot it out with at least some semblance of an even break. Slowly, painfully he crawled, avoiding clumps of grass that would stir as he passed. He covered ten yards, twenty, and judged at last that he was well to Coates's left.

With infinite care, he rolled shallowly onto his right side. Raising his head, he saw Coates studying the brush clump that he had vacated. Avoiding sudden movement, he eased up to a sitting position, he put his hands on the ground, and got ready to rise.

Maybe Coates, with a gunman's sixth sense, had become aware of Roan's intent regard. Maybe he just felt uneasy. But he turned his head, and, as his eyes met Roan's, he jerked and began to swing.

Roan forced himself to his feet. Crouching, he grabbed for his gun. Coates's rifle swung, centered on Roan's body. Roan's hand, slippery with mud, fumbled as it touched the gun grips. And now there was no time. Time had run out.

The muzzle of Coates's rifle looked enormous, black, menacing. Coates actually laughed. And then, somewhere behind Roan, a man shouted and a woman screamed. Janet, he thought, and wiped the palm of his hand on his pants leg.

He stood there, while Coates waited for him to break. The instant his hand touched his gun again, Coates would shoot. Suddenly a terrible, cold resolve formed in him. He yelled: "Shoot! Shoot and be damned!"

His hand flashed to the butt of his gun. The Colt cleared the holster and came up, fast. But Coates was faster. Roan felt the bullet before he heard the roar of the gun. He felt it, and didn't falter. His gun leveled, centered on Coates's chest, and bucked against his palm. Then he began to fall, for his left leg would not support his weight.

Falling, he thought he had missed. Coates's rifle was still up. But why didn't Coates fire again?

Roan blinked against a sudden blurring of his vision, and, when it cleared, he understood. A look of blank surprise had settled on Coates's face. All top gunmen eventually came to the belief that they were set apart from lesser men, somehow immune to death at the hands of slower opponents. And now Coates could not cope with the truth. The rifle barrel lowered slowly, as that arrogant brain accepted the inevitable. Coates folded by degrees, lay upon the ground, and was still.

Funny, Roan thought. *He fired from the hip. I guessed he forgot it wasn't a six-gun, that rifle. It threw him off.*

He crawled to Coates and got his rifle. Using it as a crutch, he boosted himself to his feet. He stared down across the valley at the flaming line camp cabin, at the three figures before it. He heard Orr shout: "Houston! Zulke! Come out here, both of you!"

He felt a touch of surprise at the change in Orr's tone. There was no inadequacy in the man now.

The uniformed man added his shout to Orr's: "Colonel Houston! I'm Captain Wilhite from Fort McBurney. I'm backing Orr to the limit, and, if I'm not enough, then a troop of cavalry will be. Come down, man, and talk!"

Houston's bellow rolled across the valley, high and defiant. "To hell with you! To hell with all of you!"

Roan drew breath into his lungs, faced the sound of Houston's voice, and shouted: "Don't count on Coates any more, Colonel! He's dead!"

For a full minute the plain was like a tomb in its utter silence. And by the silence Roan knew how very much the diminutive colonel had depended upon his deadly shadow. At last Houston yelled: "It's a lie! Coates, sing out!"

Again that silence, broken this time by the cavalry captain. "Come on, Colonel. A powwow at least!"

Roan saw Houston's short figure come erect a hundred yards away. Houston stood, proud and still for a moment, as though daring the settlers to shoot him, and Roan could not repress a stir of admiration for the man's personal courage. No shots were fired, however, and Houston stalked pompously down toward the cabin.

Zulke came into the open. Manette followed, but hung back, no longer accepting the rôle of leader of the settlers. Roan heard Wilhite call: "Colonel, there are a hundred armed men here who would like nothing better than to continue this fight! Surrender your force to me and I will escort you safely to Antelope Junction. Refuse, and I'll bring a troop of cavalry into the country and hunt down the last man who escapes the fight."

Houston asked, his voice carrying clearly in the still, cold air: "How can you guarantee safe conduct to Antelope Junction?"

The sheriff stepped toward him. "Colonel, I'm the settlers' sheriff. I add my guarantee to the captain's." He turned and looked at Zulke. "You understand, Otto? There's to be no more trouble."

Tension lay like a pall of smoke over the valley, the flames of violence curbed but not dead. Roan felt it, as each of the men in the valley surely felt it. One shot now, and slaughter was inevitable. The men beside the cabin stood rigidly, save for Manette, who was carefully rolling a cigarette, his thoughts quite apparently elsewhere.

The imminence of death had given added stature to the sheriff, but it took something out of both Houston and Zulke. They stood with heads bowed, humbled, painfully aware that, if the flames of violence leaped again, they would be among the first to die.

Orr said sharply: "Zulke, withdraw your men. Colonel, as soon as they're out of range, bring yours in."

Zulke moved back, followed by a weary Manette, and disappeared behind the cabin. Roan heard his bellowing voice and saw the settlers begin to ease back from their places of concealment. Time dripped away like water from a pump, monotonously slow, but at last they disappeared over a rise of ground.

Only then did Houston shout: "All right! Come on in, all of you!"

They came, sullenly and sheepishly, revolvers holstered, rifles pointing at the ground. Relief sighed out of Roan and he hobbled down the slight grade toward the growing group at its bottom.

Roan headed toward Janet. She was facing him, her body taut with concern. Then she was running, her father, the sheriff, all else forgotten. She raced toward him, her skirts held high so that she would not fall.

I have nothing to offer her, he thought, and then felt shame because he knew Janet would want nothing, nothing at all but her man. He propped himself solidly on the rifle crutch, and opened his arms wide to receive her.

ABOUT THE AUTHOR

Lewis B. Patten wrote more than ninety Western novels in thirty years, and three of them won Spur Awards from the Western Writers of America. The author also received the Golden Saddleman Award. Indeed, this reveals the most remarkable aspect of his work: not that there is so much of it, but that so much of it is so fine. Patten was born in Denver, Colorado, and served in the U.S. Navy, 1933–1937. He was educated at the University of Denver during the war years and became an auditor for the Colorado Department of Revenue during the 1940s. It was in this period that he began contributing significantly to Western pulp magazines, fiction that was from the beginning fresh and unique and revealed Patten's lifelong concern with the sociological and psychological affects of group psychology on the frontier. He became a professional writer at the time of his first novel, *Massacre at White River* (1952). The dominant theme in much of his fiction is the notion of justice, and its opposite, injustice. In his first novel it has to do with exploitation of the Ute Indians, but as he matured as a writer he explored this theme with significant and poignant detail in small towns throughout the early West. Crimes, such as rape or lynching, are often at the center of his stories. When the values embodied in these small towns are examined closely, they are found to be wanting. Conformity is always easier than taking a stand. Yet, in Patten's view of the American West, there is usually a man or a woman who refuses to conform. Among his finest titles, always a difficult choice, are surely *Death of a Gunfighter* (1968), *A Death in Indian Wells* (1970), and *The Law at Cottonwood* (1978). No less noteworthy are his previous Five Star Westerns, *Tincup in the Storm Country*, *Trail to Vicksburg*, *Death Rides the Denver Stage*, *The Woman at Ox-Yoke*, and *Ride the Red Trail*. His next Five Star Western will be *Savage Desert*.